MW00908226

TURN THE PAGE

By

Judy K. Wood

CHAPTER ONE

Life Lessons

It was the evenings she dreaded most, when optimism was nowhere to be found. Time would pass so slowly, and despair would make itself at home. She thought about Mrs. Mackenzie down the hall and wondered how she would be received if she knocked on her door and asked if she could visit for a while. Anytime they met in the stairway or in the laundry room, was a bright spot in her day. Mrs. Mackenzie always had something enlightening to share, and humor was part of her nature. She actually seemed to glow, and Missy was in awe of her presence. She never revealed anything about herself, her family, her past, but Missy assumed she must have led an easy, charmed life to be so centered and content.

The television across the room had been on since she finished dinner, but she had tuned it out. All those channels and nothing was on. That's what Steve used to say. He would surf forever, then say, "nothing on". She would give anything to sit through that act with him again. And, here came those thoughts. Why did it have to happen. What was she going to do now. How was she going to live out the rest of her life alone. She got up off the couch, as if moving from that spot would wipe the slate clean. But, her thoughts moved along with her, patiently waiting for an answer.

She heard a door shut next door, and a couple of thud sounds. Mr. Crawford had moved out earlier that month, to his daughter's was the assumption. He was not happy to move, but his daughter kept insisting, and for his own good. She had three little girls who loved their grandpa. Missy wished she had at least taken a phone number just to keep in touch, but he was out before she had a chance. He was a sweet old guy. Well, she figured, now he would live on for eternity in her mind. So, she wondered, who would be her new neighbor? It was a cute little apartment, just right for a single person. She had actually considered, for a very brief moment, moving in when she realized Mr. Crawford had left, but she wasn't ready. Not yet. She heard a few more bumps and bangs. She thought about going over and introducing herself, but decided she would give her new neighbor a chance to settle in. She didn't want to appear as nosy. First impressions can leave you misjudged for a long time. Just then there was a very loud crashing sound. Well, so much for first impressions. She was out of her front door and charging into the apartment next door without hesitation. She saw what looked like the body of a man on the floor of the kitchen, but it wasn't all there. She stopped quick at the sight until she heard a voice.

"I'm good, don't worry. Just fell over a box. Gimme a minute." She saw his arm reaching around until it grabbed onto a metal and plastic object on the floor near his waist. It looked like the bottom part of a leg, from a life-sized doll or something. He turned it over in his hand, got a better grasp and twisted his body until his hand reached the end of his lower extremities. She heard some clicks. He straightened out and twisted to his right side, sliding his hand down and moving his other leg to straighten it out. Then he rolled onto his side and reached both hands up onto the kitchen counter while bending the leg he had just straightened. He pulled himself up with his massive arms and upper body, and stood for a second, catching his breath. "Bet you don't see this everyday, huh. I must have made quite a ruckus. Probably scared the bejesus out of you." He reached out his hand. "Hi, I'm Jamie." Missy stepped forward and shook his hand.

"I'm Missy, I, I live next door...heard a crash."

He smiled and said, "So much for first impressions. You okay?"

Missy realized she was staring and acting like a robot. She relaxed her shoulders and said, "Oh, yes, of course, how about you?"

He smirked, "Hell yah, I've been through worse than that." She gave him a nervous smile. He didn't look much older than high school. She glanced around the apartment and couldn't help but notice the American flag folded neatly on top of one of the boxes. He observed the direction of her gaze and said, "National Guard, Iraq, second tour. Should have listened to my mom and left it at one." When she looked back at him, he was smiling again, shrugged his shoulders and said, "Shit happens." She shook her head slowly up and down.

"So, um, can I help you with anything? Do you have more boxes, or need help putting any of this away?"

"Oh, no, thanks. I have a couple of buddies stopping by tomorrow to help me get squared away. I don't have much stuff anyway." She smiled and stood for an awkward moment, then he gave her permission to exit with, "Well, nice to meet you, Missy. I'll try to keep it down from now on." She shook her head yes and then no, like no bother, and headed for the door.

She turned a bit and said, "Have a good night", pulling the door shut behind her. As she headed back into her apartment, she whispered, scolding herself, "Have a good night. How stupid."

Her head was spinning. How could he be so nonchalant? He acted as if losing a leg was no big deal. He looked so young, she couldn't imagine it had happened that long ago. He sure seemed to have adjusted quickly. She spent the rest of the night wondering. She readied for bed and got under the covers, still thinking about what she had witnessed. Without realizing it, she moved through the night without dwelling on herself, and actually slept through until morning. She awoke to the thin stream of sunlight entering through her bedroom window, finding the slightest gap in the curtains. After the long, dark night, the sunshine was blinding. She thought of the young man next door, and wondered if he was as comfortable with his handicap as he appeared, or if it was a front. If it was a front, he sure played the part well. She headed for the kitchen and started the coffee, then to her front door for the paper. When she opened the door, Mrs. Mackenzie was in the hallway. She didn't seem to be heading in any direction, but was just sort of standing there, as though she was waiting for Missy to open the door. "Good morning, Mrs. Mackenzie."

Mrs. Mackenzie smiled and simply replied, "Every morning is a good morning."

Normally, Missy would have thought "not really", but today without thinking she just said "True."

"I see we have a new neighbor moving in already."

"Yes, I actually met him last night." Missy didn't feel it was proper for her to go into detail quite yet.

"Is he a looker?" Good ole Mrs. Mackenzie. Not the first question you would expect from a woman who was probably in her eighties.

Missy smiled and said, "Yes, but he is young enough to be my son." Again, this normally would stir up sad thoughts for Missy. Not today. She moved from that comment right into her next saying, "He seemed like a very nice young man."

"Good. They're rare. Not working today, Missy?"

"Not today, it's Sunday."

"Today is Sunday? Hmmf, everyday is Sunday when you're as old as me. So, what is on your agenda for today?"

Missy hesitated for a second, and out of nowhere replied, "I was thinking of heading to the park. Not too many beautiful days left before it's too cold to spend the day outside." She thought to herself, "who am I....I haven't ever been to the park, ever." Mrs. Mackenzie smiled from ear to ear and her eyes lit up like it was Christmas.

"That sounds wonderful. It does look like a great day to go to the park. Enjoy yourself." As she turned and headed down the hall, Missy thought she could hear the elderly woman singing a tune as her head tossed back and forth.

Monday morning finally arrived. They entered the medical building for what seemed to be the hundredth time. The large windows, pastel colors and numerous potted trees in the entryway were great attempts to make the place look cheery and inviting, but no one was happy to enter. They knew just where to go, heading straight for the elevators to hit the button marked with a 5, where they would turn right, walking on a floor that had been polished to infinity, and through the doors to #502C. The waiting room was empty. They had learned the first appointment of the day was the best time to avoid a long wait. The receptionist behind the glass smiled and nodded. A minute later the door to the offices opened, and Dr. Lew himself stood with a file in his hand and summoned them in with a smile. This was it. They had been through all of her treatments, therapies, prescriptions and ill affects from each of them. Now they would find out if it was all worth it. They followed him into his office and as he moved to his chair behind the desk he quickly announced, "All clear." As the three of them settled into their chairs he continued with the good news. Kim and Brent were in as much of a fog hearing this good news as they had been twelve months ago when he was delivering the bad. Just as they did back then, they had to focus to take in all that he was saying. They felt like they were underwater and everything was being said too fast, and too slow at the same time. Dr. Lew finished with his delivery, one which he always preferred over the alternative, and asked if they had any questions. They both drew a blank, and it was all Brent could do not to break down and join Kim with her tears of relief and joy. He promised himself throughout her treatment that if she were to survive this, he would be a better husband. No more golfing weekends with the guys, staying at the office far into the night, and for sure, he was going to stop drinking so much. So, she survived. Now what.

An appointment was set for follow-up a few months later that year and they left the building. She reached for his hand, but he was fumbling for his keys, as though he didn't always drop them in his right pants pocket.

The first time Brent ever saw her was when he was a junior at Penn State. She was looking for her roommates in the bleachers at one of his wrestling matches. Their eyes met for a second, and she blushed and headed up through the crowd to the top row where all the "in" girls sat. From then on, he seemed to notice her everywhere he went on campus. He later joked with her that she was stalking him, though they both knew it ended up being the other way around. They were voted "Best Looking Couple" at a graduation party, and at their wedding, everyone remarked that they looked better than the figurines on top of their wedding cake. With some financial help from Kim's father, he opened his own Chiropractic office, while she worked alongside him as a massage therapist and ran the tanning studio. The money was good, and suited their lifestyle with plenty of time to look after themselves, and that they did. Their year-round tanned skin was offset by the latest in hairstyles, weekly facials, pedicures and manicures. They spent most of their free time at the gym or heading into the city to shop for the latest fashion trends.

Time passed, as it does when you aren't paying attention. Brent started to spend more time on the golf course and Kim headed to the casinos in Atlantic City on weekend trips with her girlfriends. They were living together, but apart. They drew every last penny out of the business, and spent it faster than it came in. Just as things were about to spin out of control, Kim got the news. For some, cancer is a challenge to discover their strength, for others a battle than cannot be won. It is a time to find out who you are, what really matters in your life, and who cares about you the most. Kim felt like they had been given a second chance, but she wasn't sure if Brent felt the same way. He certainly supported her throughout her ordeal, but now she wondered if they would fall back into the same empty lifestyle, or move forward with a better appreciation for each other and the life they had been given.

"You hungry? Want to grab something to eat somewhere?" Brent asked, looking straight ahead as they pulled away from the curb.

"I'm not very hungry, just kind of tired. I didn't sleep much last night. Let's just go home and I can fix us something."

He shrugged and continued to drive. As they got closer to their block, they heard sirens and were passed by an ambulance and two police cars. When they approached their intersection, there were police cars blocking their avenue, so they stopped as a police officer directing traffic approached the car. "Can't turn up there. We have an apartment building on fire. Gonna have to continue on."

"Do you know what building it is? We live at The Commons."

The policeman sighed. "You might want to park it here then. I'm afraid it's your building. I'll get a firefighter over here to escort you to the building." He followed through on his radio and within minutes a young man in full gear trudged over and nodded for them to join him.

"Fire's out. It was just one apartment. Luckily, it was in the front corner so we were able to contain it. No one was hurt. We got everyone in the building out, and the people weren't home in the burnt out unit." They were within sight of the building now and could see the crowd of tenants corralled by one of the firetrucks in the shade.

"Oh God, no." Kim was the first to blurt out. She covered the lower part of her face with both hands. Brent just kept walking, his eyes focused on their corner apartment. Then he released a deep moaning sigh.

The firefighter turned and looked at them. "It's yours? Oh, I'm sorry, folks. I'll bring you over to the Chief."

As they followed him to the man dressed in street clothes with a firefighter hat and a bullhorn, they noticed the other tenants all staring at them, some shaking their heads, all with looks of sympathy. For the second time that day, they felt like they were underwater, and had to focus on what was being said to them. But, this time, it was not what they wanted to hear. "You the folks from 1B? We couldn't save it. It was all we could do to keep it from spreading. We'll have a full report shortly from our inspector, but it looked like it started in the kitchen, most likely at the gas range. Did you use it at all this morning?"

Brent's head dropped like it was about to fall off his shoulders. He sighed again and without raising his head, shook a slow "yes" response. "I was going to cook up some eggs, and then saw we didn't have any bread for toast, so I just...I, I don't think I went back to the stove to turn the burner off. Oh, God. I can't believe it. I can't believe it."

"Well, no one was hurt. That's the important thing. Your insurance should cover the contents, and probably provides coverage for you to stay somewhere until you can move back in. You should call your agent right away. They can probably arrange to put you up in a hotel for tonight."

Brent had moved his focus from his chest to a spot on the sidewalk about three feet away. When the Chief finished his recommendation, Brent started shaking his head from side to side.

Then he turned his gaze to Kim. She knew instantly what he was about to say and her eyes flashed at him. "Don't tell me. No."

"I kept waiting for the credit card balance to go down so I could call it in to the insurance. Then I figured we could just skip it this year. We've been paying the rental insurance for years, and it was just money out the window. I never thought...." Brent's face was red and his hands were trembling as he ran them through his hair. "I never...."

Mrs. Mackenzie had been standing at the edge of the tenant crowd grasping a sweater flung over her shoulders, and now was making her way through the maze of police cars and firetrucks with Missy right behind her. Without saying a word, Mrs. Mackenzie approached Kim and gave her a hug. "I'm so sorry for both of you. I called 911 when I smelled the smoke, and they were here within minutes, but I'm afraid it was too late. They told us we can go back in later, once they make sure it is safe. Do you folks have somewhere to stay tonight?" Kim shook her head, no, while tears welled up in her tired eyes.

Missy spoke up. "You can stay with me. I have an extra room, and you are welcome to it for as long as you need a place to stay." Missy had never officially met the couple from 1B, but had crossed paths with them many times over the years. She had always thought they were a bit full of themselves. They barely acknowledged her when she greeted them, and never initiated any greeting themselves, but now they were people in need, stuck-up or not, she was happy to make the offer.

Kim looked at Brent, who still avoided eye contact with her and replied to Missy, "Thank you so much. That is very kind of you. We may just have to take you up on your offer. It seems we don't have insurance." There was a long pause of silence, with everyone looking at each other and then looking away, except for Brent. He was still focusing on that spot on the sidewalk.

He slowly looked at Missy. To his knowledge, this was the first time he had ever laid eyes on her. "Do you live in our building?"

"Oh, yes, I'm in 1D."

Awkward silence was finally interrupted by the Chief who said, "Well, we'll be finishing up here and then I'm going to have some paperwork for you sign, and a statement and such. Uh, where is it best to reach you?"

Brent robotically reached in his back pocket, pulled out his wallet and removed a business card. He handed it to the Chief and said, I'm there Monday through Friday. If I'm with a patient just leave a voicemail and I'll get right back to you."

Kim, Brent, Mrs. Mackenzie and Missy stood on one side of the street and the other tenants stood across the street. Missy had seen her new neighbor, Jamie, and his friends when they were evacuated, but they seemed to have left just before she crossed the street with Mrs. Mackenzie. She noticed they all had the same buzz-cut, clean-cut look as Jaimie, and assumed they must have served with him.

Finally, the emergency vehicles started pulling out one at a time and their street looked like their street again, except for the yellow tape stringing from tree trunk to tree trunk at the corner of the building and a couple of orange and white sawhorses on the sidewalk. They were given the all-clear and the larger crowd started filing into the building. Once the last of them passed through the door, Mrs. Mackenzie and Missy headed across the street. Brent and Kim didn't move until Missy turned back and said, "Come on. Let's go inside."

The apartment door was shut with streams of the same yellow tape criss-crossing the doorframe. Kim and Brent were anxious to go inside. The Chief told them the investigation was completed and they could enter when they wanted, but he had warned them there wasn't much that was salvageable. They weren't prepared for what they saw when they opened the door. It looked like a bomb had gone off. Everything was wet and black. Furniture was overturned and burnt. They both started coughing as the toxic smell of melted plastic and smoke hung in the air. The curtains hung in shreds around broken windows. They stood in the doorway to the kitchen and barely recognized it as their own. No, nothing looked salvageable. It was hard to believe that the fire could have been so devastating to their place, and the rest of the building was not damaged. They turned to leave and joined Mrs. Mackenzie and Missy who had waited out in the hallway. When Mrs. Mackenzie got to her door she said, "I'll check on you folks in a bit." She nodded her head and gave a slight smile to Missy, then closed the door behind her.

"Let's get you settled in, and I'll fix you something to eat." Missy unlocked her door and stepped back for her neighbors to enter first. They carried with them the smell of their burnt possessions, even though they had only been in the apartment for a matter of minutes. "Make yourself at home. The bathroom is over there and my son's.....um, your room is right next door." She turned into her kitchen entryway. That was the first time she had to refer to Jason's room out loud, and it had rolled off her tongue like nothing had ever happened. She tossed the thought from her mind and started to make busy with food.

Brent finally looked at Kim. "I can't tell you how sorry I am, Kim. I can't believe what I have done to you. After all you've been through. I can't believe I have done this. And, the insurance..." His voice dropped off.

Kim turned to him and took his hands, still trembling, in hers. She looked him straight in the eye and he returned her gaze. "The fire was an accident. I could have done the same thing. We both knew the insurance and some of our other bills were piling up. Don't blame yourself. No one was hurt. We'll start again. We are together. We have our health." At this point he started sobbing, shoulders shaking, tears streaming down his face. Kim held his hands more tightly. "We're going to be fine. We can't change what happened, or who we had become, but we can do better in the future. Maybe this will be the start of a whole new life for us. Between the news I got today, and this fire, I actually feel like we are going to start new, start fresh, and appreciate what we have together."

"How can you say that? We have nothing. Nothing."

Kim moved her hands from his hands to his shoulders and gave him a strong shake. "We have more than most. We have each other. And we can do this." Brent shook his head up and down.

"We beat cancer, didn't we. We can do anything." They hugged each other so tight they both stopped breathing.

Kathryn hoped she would catch him before he left the office. She knew he had had a long day, and was probably looking forward to getting out of there. He picked up the phone on the second ring.

"You coming home soon? I have a nice dinner started for you." Kathryn knew how to put a smile on his face.

"I'm heading out now. Long day. The meeting lasted forever. I'll tell you more about it when I get home, but basically, they want to have all six stores conform to the same floor plan. They say people will be more apt to visit our stores if they are all laid out the same way. I understand their thinking, but I know they aren't going to like paying the bill to get such an undertaking accomplished." He sighed heavily into the phone. "This is like starting all over again, and I'm getting too old for this. Anyway, I'll see you in a bit. Do you need me to stop on my way home for anything?"

"No, I'm all set. Oh, there's a message on the machine from your music publisher. Just said to call him back today." Keith had been writing country songs since he was a teenager. That was actually how Kathryn met him. He used to play at all the corner bars, and she used to round up her friends to end up wherever he was playing. He used to keep an eye on the door, hoping the pretty young thing with a blond braid and bright blue eyes would show up. He eventually got the nerve to tip his hat one evening in her direction and she lit up like the

4th of July. They had been "magic" ever since. Of course, when they announced their engagement her father sat her down and told her Keith was a nice young man, but he needed a real job. He set Keith up in one of his grocery stores with a position in management. It was a good job, but took up a lot of his time. He stopped playing, and only wrote a song occasionally. He moved up the ladder of positions until he was in charge of all three stores owned by Kathryn's father. Her father then sold out to a major chain, and Keith was not only able to keep his job, but continued to get promoted to his present position. He was grateful for the comfortable life they were able to live, but missed writing and performing.

"O.K., I'll call Jack on my way home. I revamped one of my old songs to bring it up to date and sent it over to him a month or so ago. You know country has to sound like rap now to get anyone's attention. No one wants to listen to the old stuff anymore, not since they dropped the western in country western. Oh, hey, did you hear from your sister today?" Kathryn's sister had been battling cancer for about a year, and today she was to get results of her last set of tests to find out if she had won.

"I didn't hear from her, so I called her a little while ago and it was strange, the phone just rang and rang. Her machine didn't pick up. I'm going to try her again in a bit. Thanks for asking. See you soon. Love you."

Keith threw his briefcase and jacket in the back seat and turned his cell phone on. There was a message from Jack, his publisher. He started his SUV, turned on the bluetooth device and dialed Jack's number without listening to the message. Jack answered as Keith pulled out of his parking lot, the last car out, as usual. "Hey, Jack, it's Keith Barron. Sorry I didn't call earlier. I was in meetings all day. What's up?"

"You are, Keith. Guess you didn't listen to my message. That last song you sent really got my attention. I took the liberty of having a couple of guys I know do a demo, and sent it to a few contacts. I got some great responses to it. Are you ready?" Keith wanted to hear more before he committed to excitement, so he didn't reply, but waited for Jack to continue. "You know the deal with the Drake brothers. They were on top of the country charts for two years, and then decided to go their separate ways. Now they compete to see who gets up there again every time they each release a new song. I think they actually time them to be able to have a fair race. Well, they both want to do your song. Looks like Aaron Drake is going to sing back up for Troy Drake and vice-versa. They each have their own sound, so it should be cool to see what they each do with your song. It gets better. Dimension Productions, you know, the movie producers, is finishing up shooting a western that is supposed to be the real deal on the Younger brothers, and they want your song, sung by Aaron at the beginning of the movie and then Troy's version at the end. This is it, Keith. I'm getting the paperwork together now for copywriting and licensing. Heh, heh, you're going to get to quit your day job, that's for sure."

Keith was speechless. He was letting it all sink in, but couldn't believe what he had heard. "I don't know what to say. I never really expected..."

"Well, expect it. Call me tomorrow and we'll set up a meeting to go over all the paperwork. You have yourself a good night."

Kathryn finished setting the table, turned off the television on the kitchen counter, and turned on some music, waiting for Keith to pull in the driveway. After the day he had, she wanted to help him relax once he walked in the door. She felt as though she had spent the entire day at the stove or washing dishes. She volunteered at the local food bank where they served meals to the homeless. She looked forward to Mondays because she got to spend time with Mrs. Mackenzie, a kind and gentle soul who called each recipient by their first name when serving them their meal. She seemed to know something personal about each one. "How are your allergies today, Bob? Here you go, Phil, and I have some scraps in the back for that pooch of yours, so finish what's on your plate here and don't go savin' any for him. Is that a new hat, Joe? You look like a million bucks." It amazed Kathryn how she knew so much about these people of the street, and remembered their names. She was a saint, making those who are normally ignored by society, feel like somebody special. Kathryn checked her watch and decided to try calling her sister one more time before it was too late in the evening to call, but then she saw the headlights growing in the driveway and went to the side door to greet Keith. He jumped out of the car and just about ran to the door, bursting it open and lunging for Kathryn. He snatched her right up off her feet and spun her around and around. She clutched onto him for fear of falling and finally planted her feet to stop the ride, laughing the entire time.

"What?" she asked. This started the hoisting up and spinning dance all over again.

Jamie made his way up the stairs to the second floor. The smell of smoke still permeated the building. He turned his head to view the door of the apartment attacked by fire and noted the yellow tape had been pulled away to allow entrance. He knocked, but no one answered. He thought Missy might know where their neighbors were, since she had been speaking with them when he and his boys left. He knocked on her door and upon its opening, saw Brent and Kim sitting in the living room. Missy greeted him and moved aside, correctly assuming he was here to see her guests. "Hi, I'm Jamie. I live next door, just moved in. I'm sorry about the fire."

Brent remained seated, but Kim moved forward to the edge of her seat and said "Oh, thank you. I'm Kim and this is my husband, Brent."

Jamie reached his hand out, offering up a plastic bag with items that just about filled it. "I brought you some things. The base has a stash of toothbrushes, shampoos, soaps and other stuff for us, and I figured you might be needing them to get through the night, wherever you're staying."

"Oh, Jamie, that is so nice of you. Come on in. I was just fixing something to eat. You hungry?" asked Missy. She closed the door as he stepped inside and made his way over to hand Kim the bag. Brent watched Jamie's awkward gate, then looked away so it wouldn't be noticed he was staring. Jamie was all too familiar with this reaction, but dismissed it as always.

"Actually, we ordered some breakfast sandwiches this morning from the corner bakery, and I'm still pretty full, but thank you for the offer, mamm." He turned his attention to Brent. "So, uh, my buddies had just helped me move the rest of my stuff in when the alarms went off. We were outside when you arrived. We figured you were the ones who lived in the apartment when you were talking to the Fire Chief. Then Mrs. Mackenzie whispered in my ear that you had no insurance. My buddies are all active-duty, settin' up to head out on their next tour of duty, but right now they all have some time to kill. We're available to start getting your place back to being live-able. We can clean out what isn't salvageable. One of the guys has a truck to haul shit, uh, stuff away, and my buddy, Chris, is a carpenter. Just cost you materials. We could start in the morning, if you want. Be glad to help you out, sir."

Jamie couldn't read Brent's face to know if his offer was being accepted or not, but Kim's chin was trembling and a tear slid down her face. She looked at Brent, who shook his head and admitted, "I don't know what to say. That is a very generous offer. I would want to pay you, but not sure right now how we could."

"No, we won't take any money. That's the deal. We like projects that are constructive. It's, you know, good."

Missy stood silently by, but she couldn't stop thinking about something Jamie had just said. He had said that Mrs. Mackenzie whispered in his ear that they had no insurance. She hadn't heard that until the two ladies had crossed the street and Brent had admitted it to the Fire Chief and his wife. While the conversation between her old and new neighbors now continued, she was aware of what was being said, but still puzzled by how Mrs. Mackenzie knew they weren't insured, or if she had the timing wrong, but it just wasn't adding up.

Brent made arrangements to connect up at 7:00 the next morning to go through the apartment and assess what could be done. Jamie nodded his head and thanked Missy again for the offer of something to eat, and left as awkwardly as he had entered.

He felt good. If someone had told him a few years ago of today's scenario, he would have cursed at them in disbelief. His life sure had turned around.

He had barely graduated high school when he got caught up with the wrong crowd. He drank, stole cigarettes, and rode around in cars his friends "borrowed from strangers". He used the term "friends" loosely, fully aware they would hang him out to dry in a heartbeat if they ever got in real trouble. The police delivered him home one night, and told his father Jamie better change his ways and his friends, or the next time they would be delivering him to the police station instead. He and his father had a screaming match that night while his mother sat in the kitchen crying. His father kicked him out of the house and told him not to return until he got his shit together. He had nowhere to go, so he started crashing with friends, and spent more than a few nights sleeping behind a dumpster in the school parking lot. One night he snuck into the cinema, hoping just to get warm and catch some sleep in a comfortable seat. He was heading into one of the theaters when an elderly lady appeared from nowhere and told him that that movie had already started, redirecting him across the hall to another theater. "This is where you want to go." she had said, pointing a large black flashlight in the direction she had turned him. He looked back over his shoulder while he was entering the recommended theater as the doorway light reflected off her brass pin, bearing the name "Mackenzie". Then she sort of disappeared into the darkness of the hallway.

As the previews were being shown, he found a seat where a tub of popcorn had been left with most of its contents, as well as a large soda, also leftover. He picked up the containers and finished them off. About six guys piled in the door and sat in the row in front of him, leaving an empty seat between each of them. He figured they must all be cops from their buzzed cuts and the way they were dressed. They were joking and messing with one another, targeting popcorn at each other's heads, calling each other names, and laughing easily. The movie started with the volume so loud, Jamie figured he'd never be able to fall asleep in here.

The movie, Black Hawk Down, was a modern day war movie, and it had him from the moment it started. He only took his eyes off the screen now and then to observe the reactions of the guys in front of him. They weren't cops, they were military. Not one muscle moved between the six of them through the entire movie. Before it was over, Jamie knew exactly what he was going to do. He was sitting on the step of the recruiter's office the next morning, waiting for them to open. He enlisted, and headed straight to his parents' house with the paperwork he had just signed. When his father opened their front door he kept any expression from showing on his face, unsure of why his son was there. Jamie held out the papers and his father looked them over, pulled his son in through the doorway and hugged him, barely able to get out the words, "Welcome home, son." His mother went into the kitchen, sat down at the table and cried.

Over the next months, Jamie went through basic training and ended up in Iraq, where he felt he belonged. His unit went out on daily patrols to the area surrounding their base, sometimes in armored vehicles, and sometimes on foot. Day after day, they let their presence be known to the locals, some of whom they knew were waiting for any opportunity to kill an American. The bond he had with the guys he served with was unlike anything he had ever experienced. They would give their life for him, and he would do the same. They were closer than brothers, they were one. His tent mate, Ben, was his best bud. When it came time to re-up, they didn't hesitate. After a short visit home, they ended up together in the same unit again, but this time they were in a hell-hole. The area they were to patrol was strong with Al-Queda. Their base was constantly under attack, and they only traveled in tanks and Humvees, never on foot. Ben had started counting down the number of days until he was supposed to go home. He was married with two boys and a third child on the way. Jamie teased him when he admitted he was hoping for a little girl this time. That's when

Jamie started calling him "Mr. Softee". As much as he was glad for Ben to go home and be with his family, he was also selfishly dreading it. It was getting late in the day when they were heading back from a patrol only 12 days before Ben was to leave. Just outside of their compound, the Humvee sputtered and halted.

"Who the fuck was supposed to fuel up this machine?" called out the driver. No one answered, but they decided they were so close to their base they could hoof it back, grab some gas and be back in before dark. They emptied out of the vehicle and scanned 360 degrees. All was quiet and serene with the exception of a group of kids playing soccer inside a chain link fence adjacent to the base. As they neared their entrance, Ben saw a soccer ball that must have escaped the game down in a ditch. He slid down the short banking and reached down to retrieve it. As he was lifting it up, Jamie noticed some heavy tape stuck to the underside of the ball, with a thin string running down into the dirt. There was no time to warn Ben. Jamie jumped down into the ditch and pushed Ben away with all of his might. Ben was still rolling away when the IED exploded, tossing Jamie up in the air like a rag doll. His ears were ringing from the blast and he was seeing spots and flashes. He was on his back, unable to move, when he felt someone on either side of him pull him up by his armpits. From what he could tell, they were running full bore as his tailbone bounced along the dirt road.

The next thing he knew, he was waking up to the sound of a helicopter. He opened his eyes and saw two medics leaning over him, except he was watching from above. He looked down and between the synchronized movements of the medics, inserting needles and hanging bags over him, one filled with blood and another of a clear liquid, he saw his own face. It was ashen white and his eyelids were half-closed with his eyeballs rolling upward. He heard one of them yelling "We're going to lose him if we don't get this pig down on the ground ASAP!"

The pilot yelled back, "Putting her down now!" While Jamie continued to watch his body being tended to, he felt the presence of someone next to him. He looked to his right and saw his Uncle Gus, dressed in Army fatigues, also focused on Jamie's body below. As the medics grabbed onto the side handles of the stretcher, he felt himself being pulled back down to join his body, and then all went black again.

The next week or two were a blur, but he ended up spending a month or so at a hospital in Germany, and then returned back to the United States where he spent the rest of that year at Bethesda. His doctors were amazed at his attitude and determination during his recovery, and especially through his physical therapy, while learning to walk again. Ben came to visit him once a month from the west coast. He tried to thank Jamie with each visit, but Jamie would put his hand up and tell Ben, "No, don't say it. You would do the same for me. Do not thank me." On their first visit Jamie had told Ben that he believed he was put on this earth for a reason, and this was part of the plan. "I don't know how to explain it, but you were supposed to pick up that ball and I was supposed to take the hit for you. I'm good with that. Your family needed you, and you needed me. It's all part of some big plan." He felt that with every bone he had left in his body. It felt good.

Kathryn woke up to the obnoxious buzzing of her alarm clock. Her head was heavy with a headache, and her stomach wasn't feeling so great either. Once Keith shared his news with her, they decided a celebration was in order. They recalled a couple of bottles of champagne down in the basement, so Keith popped the plastic cork while Kathryn pulled out the fluted glasses she had been saving from their wedding. They toasted country music. They toasted Jack - the best publisher ever. They toasted the Drake brothers. They toasted the Younger brothers. By the time they opened the second bottle, they were toasting the moon, the carpet, and the dog, even though they didn't have a dog. It was all a bit foggy now, but Kathryn recalled it was one hell of a night. She slowly got out of bed and headed for the bathroom. She could hear Keith downstairs, making coffee and using the toaster, quite loudly in her opinion. She threw back some aspirin and chased it down with bathroom tap water collected in her hand. Desperate times called for desperate measures. As she entered the kitchen, Keith was dressed for the office, whistling and pouring them each a cup of hot coffee. He gave her a big smile. "How you doing, Tiger?", he asked while handing her a cup.

"I've been better. Haven't been this hung over since I went to Atlantic City with Kim. Oh my God, Kim. I have to call her this morning. I'm afraid she didn't get good news yesterday." She reached for the phone and dialed her sister's number. Again, as yesterday, the phone just rang, with no answering machine service. She pulled her cell phone from her purse on the counter and tried Kim's cell. No answer, but she was able to leave a voicemail. She decided to get dressed and drive over to Kim's apartment, knowing she never left for work before 9:00.

When she arrived at The Commons, she first saw the yellow tape still clinging to the trees out front, then she saw the smashed windows. Her heart sank. She actually thought she might be ill. She ran up the stairway and in the front door. Once inside she could hear Kim's voice coming from the apartment door which was ajar. She stepped through the doorway and could not believe what she was seeing. Kim was standing in the middle of chaos. There were young men dumping debris in a large pile while Kim was calling out to someone in the kitchen saying, "Good, at least I'll have a pot to piss in."

Someone out in the hallway called out, "Chris is here with the truck!", and the men stopped what they were doing to each take sides of furniture and exit the apartment. Kim turned and saw her sister moving out of their way, and burst into tears.

They ran to each other and hugged, both sobbing. "Oh my God, Kim, what happened?" Kim gave Kathryn the short version of the story, seeing no good reason to tell her that it was Brent's fault, and holding back on their lapse in insurance for now. Kathryn had always let Kim know that she disapproved of their lifestyle, and warned her more than once that things have a way of catching up with you. She knew Kathryn would not be so insensitive to give her the I-told-you-so speech at this moment, but Kim knew she would be thinking it. "I've been trying to call you since last night. Did you go to your appointment yesterday?!

"That was just yesterday? Seems like longer than that. Yes, and I'm clear." She smiled, revealing her beautiful set of teeth, whitened a shade too light by Kathryn's standards, but that was Kim.

"Oh, thank God. Would be terrible if you had to deal with bad news and then this." They looked around at the apartment. Since Jamie's friends had started removing the worst of the debris, the living room actually wasn't looking so bad. They had pulled the carpeting up, and the hardwood floor underneath actually looked pretty good. Jamie was washing down the walls, and his friend Chris was removing the windows to bring into town to have the broken glass replaced. Their bedroom door had been shut at the time of the fire, so other than a good spring cleaning, it was in pretty good shape. The worst room, of course, was the kitchen. As they entered, Kim looked around and saw Mrs. Mackenzie was gone.

"Guess she stepped out. I wanted to introduce you to my neighbor. She is the sweetest lady. Came right over and gave me a big hug yesterday when we first arrived and saw what had happened. She's been trying to help me more than you can imagine. It's just such a disaster." Actually, Kim was a bit relieved, as she wasn't sure how to introduce her neighbor to her sister. She didn't know her neighbor's name. This morning Mrs. Mackenzie had greeted Kim and Brent, calling them by their first names. Kim couldn't get herself to ask the woman what her name was after all this time. She kept hoping Missy or Jamie would say her name, but so far, Jamie only called her Mamm.

Kathryn took a deep breath. "Well, I can pick up in here." She looked over at the gas stove and the burnt out cabinets above. "Is that what started it? You should see if something was faulty with it before they haul it out of here.

Course, your insurance should cover for a new one, so I guess it doesn't matter." Kim didn't reply, but just shrugged her shoulders. The two women started a pile for the guys to take to the landfill, and sorted what could be saved. To avoid any more questions about the fire or insurance, Kim decided to direct the conversation towards Kathryn.

"So, how is everything with you? Did Brent have that big meeting you were telling me about?"

Kathryn thought twice before answering. She saw no good reason to tell her sister that Brent's job was no longer a concern, that they were about to strike it rich in the music industry and were going to be living the good life. So, she held back and explained the grocery chain's decision to have duplicate floor plans in all of their stores. If she had known that there was no recovery through insurance, she definitely would have shared the good fortune news and offered to help Kim and Brent get back on their feet. Even though she didn't approve of their lifestyle, she loved her sister and would help her in anyway she could.

"So, where are you staying, Kim? Where did you stay last night?"

"Well, it turns out we have incredible neighbors. The woman across the hall, Missy, invited us to stay with her, in her son's room. He must be away at school or something. And, the guy in the living room, the one washing down the walls, he is our neighbor too. His name is Jamie. He just moved in. And then there is an older lady."

Before Kim could explain that she didn't know the older lady's name, Kathryn looked over her shoulder and called out, "Mrs. Mackenzie? What are you doing here?"

"Oh my goodness, hello Kathryn. I live down the hall. What are you doing here?"

"You know each other?" Kim asked, glancing between her sister and her neighbor. The three women were all looking at each other and giggling.

Jamie and Chris entered the kitchen. "Hey", Jamie announced, "Chris told the guy at the glass place about the fire and that you're paying for this out of your pocket 'cause you don't have insurance, so the guy said he's only gonna charge you what it cost him for the glass. He's not going to charge you for his labor. Sweet, huh?"

Mrs. Mackenzie had intentionally left when Kathryn arrived. She had seen no reason for the sisters to know that she was in on both of their lives up until now. She had hoped that Kim would confess the full details of the fire, and Kathryn would share her good news and ability to help. But, since that didn't happen, she arranged for another good deed to move things in the proper direction.

Kathryn looked at her sister. "Why is he saying you don't have insurance?" Kim looked ashamed and in front of everyone admitted to her sister that they hadn't paid their premium and the policy was cancelled. She felt her face redden as she waited for Kathryn's reaction.

Kathryn walked over to her sister and took her hand. She led her into the living room where they could be alone and told her everything was going to be O.K. She told Kim about Keith's song, and said, "I am so sorry that you felt you couldn't tell me about the insurance. You know how much I love you. This is the plan. Once you figure out exactly what you need here, you and I are going on a shopping spree, and I'm going to replace everything you have lost. Keith and I can well-afford it now, and I am happy to help you, so please, don't worry. O.K.?"

Kim took a deep breath. As tears once again streamed down her cheeks, she told her sister of her conversation with Brent, that they were going to start a new life. She declared to Kathryn, "You will see. I think we've been given a second chance to do things right. We're starting over, and we're going to be better people. We are." Kathryn knew her sister better than anyone, and when she said she was going to do something, she did it. She never felt closer to her than she did at that moment. Everything was going to be O.K..

When Missy left work she decided she better make a quick stop on the way home to pick up a few things for dinner. She had decided a pasta dinner would be easy, and everyone likes pasta. She was heading over to the baked goods for some nice bread when she spotted Mr. Crawford's daughter. She had met his daughter several times when he was living next door. Missy approached the young woman and gave a tentative hello. She wasn't sure if the daughter would recognize her. "Oh, hello, Missy, right?"

"Yes, that's right. How is your father doing? I didn't get to say goodbye before he moved out. Is he staying with you?" The blank expression she was looking into said it all.

"My father passed away the day after we moved him into my house. He died in his sleep. He was fine when we all went to bed, but in the morning I went in to check on him. It was going on 10:00 and I knew he didn't sleep in that late. He was gone."

"I am so sorry." Missy said, though she remembered that these words were of little comfort to her when she heard them herself.

"Well, he's with my sister now. She passed ten years ago, and I know Dad never got over it. We decided to just have a private service for him. All of his friends are already gone."

"He was a nice man. You were lucky to have him in your life as long as you did. How are your girls handling it?"

The daughter nodded her head to one side and said, "They're young. They don't really understand it all. I guess they are lucky in that way. And, how is your family?"

Missy stopped breathing. "I, they, um, all good, thanks. Well, I have to get going, I'm sorry about your father. You take care." She abandoned her cart of items and left the store. Once in her car, she sat at the wheel with the keys in her hand. It had been two years. She still couldn't talk about it. She thought about Mr. Crawford's grand daughters being too young to understand it all. She was 47 and didn't understand it either. Her husband and son were such good people. Steve taught math and English at a local magnet school. He stayed late for any of the kids that needed extra help. Her son was a great kid. He volunteered on weekends at the animal shelter. Why did their lives have to be cut short, and the drunk driver that killed them gets to live. It was so senseless. She had baked cookies that night and they were out of milk. Steve asked Jason if he wanted to drive to help get some hours in before he took the test. They should have only been a few minutes, but she didn't notice the time until she heard the sirens. As Missy sat in her car, reliving that night, a man walked by, limping. He had a cast on his left foot. It reminded her of her new neighbor, who had taken what life gave him and continued on, appreciating each day and

42

doing for others. He didn't sit around feeling sorry for himself. And then she thought of the other couple in her building who had just lost everything. Curious how they had all been thrown together. She thought maybe there was a plan, and she had to start participating in life again if she wanted to be part of it. She started her car and headed home.

As she climbed the stairs, she heard music and it seemed as though it was coming from her apartment. She opened her door and found Kim and Kathryn busy in the kitchen, and whatever they were working on was making her mouth water. Kim wheeled around and gave Missy a big smile. "Welcome home. We figured you would like a nice dinner waiting for you after a hard day at work. Kim introduced her sister who offered a glass of wine from one of the bottles she had brought from home. Missy took her up on the offer. They said dinner would be ready in a bit, and their husbands were on the way. They hoped Missy didn't mind, but they also invited Jamie to join them, to thank him for his help at Kim's apartment. Kim said they would probably be able to start staying in their own place in a couple of days. Missy surprised herself by being a little saddened that they wouldn't be staying longer, but understood they were anxious to be in their own place. Brent and Keith arrived a few minutes later, knocking on Jamie's door as they passed to let him know dinner was ready.

It was a grand evening. Good food, and some good laughter at the expense of the sisters who were very competitive, but in a fun way. Keith had brought his guitar and sang a few songs, urging them to join him for each chorus. Jamie even tried to teach Brent some line dancing moves. Missy loved Kim's sister. She was so down to earth and very funny. She invited Missy to join her on her next trip to a local apple orchard to pick apples. It seemed they had all needed a good night.

Chris picked up the windows at the glass repair shop, and as promised, they only charged for the materials used. There were still good people in this world. He loaded them into the back of his truck and started heading to Jamie's to see if they could get them installed. He decided to stop on the way and see if his brother was home. He had lost his job, so it was a pretty sure bet he'd be there. "Willie, it's me. Open the door." Chris called out after knocking on the front and back doors. He could hear loud music coming from the kitchen and the television was blaring in the living room, so he had to pound with his fist and shout through the door. Finally, he heard the deadbolt unlock and the door was opened just an inch or two. He pushed the rest of the way and caught a glimpse of his brother, wearing white sox and blue boxers shuffling away, down the hall. Chris entered and immediately turned the radio off and searched for the television remote, which wasn't easy with the mess of the place. He finally hit the power button on the television, and the overload of sound halted. His brother exited the bathroom and acted surprised to see him.

"Oh, hey Chris. How you doin', man? Whassup?" Willie looked like hell, as usual. Chris assumed he hadn't showered, or even gotten dressed in days. He certainly hadn't brushed his teeth or his hair. Shaving would have required even more effort, so that project had slipped for a few weeks according to his stubble-to-beard growth. "I was just getting ready to head out, run some errands and stuff. So, how are you doin' man? You look good."

Chris waited for him to stop talking and said, "Go take a shower. You got any clean clothes? Put them on. We're going to have a talk, but I can't stand looking at you until you clean yourself up. You stink, man." Willie had no response, just turned around and headed back into the bathroom. Chris leaned against the wall in the hallway and waited. When his brother opened the bathroom door, he still looked disgusting, but at least he was cleaner. "You look like Dad." Chris decided to jump right in and let Willie have it. "Remember when we came home from school everyday, and Dad would be on the couch, in his underwear, all sloppy and drunk?

45

We used to go to our rooms and lock the door until Mom got home from work. Remember, Willie? Well, that is who you have become. You are wasting your life the way Dad did. I bet Mom is turning over in her grave right now. You have no life, no friends and only one family member that gives a shit about you, and that is me. So, here's the deal. You are going to clean this shit hole up today. I have to go do something, and when I come back I'm going to stay here until you dry out, so get a room ready for me. You have two weeks until I ship out to Iraq, so get your ass in gear. Did you get all that, or do I have to repeat it for you?" Chris had moved closer and was in Willie's face, which had turned solemn.

"I'm sorry, Chris. I know I'm a loser. You're the good one, always have been." was Willie's only reply.

"Do you want to be a loser? You can be anything you want to be, ain't nothin' stoppin' you but yourself. You can be the good one. Just keep away from that fucking bottle. Don't let it take your life away. You're a talented guy. I've never seen anyone can take an entire truck apart and put it back together like you can. I promise you that if you get back on track, life will be so much better than sitting around here in your own stench in a drunken stupor. Hell, you might even get Jillian back. I saw her last week, and hand-up-to-God, she asked about you and said she missed you, she just couldn't deal with your drinking anymore. Man, I know it won't be easy, but it'll be worth it, Your life just sucks right now. Am I right?"

Willie looked him square in the eyes. "You'll help me? You know the rough part will be the next few days. I've done it before. Went three years without a drink 'til Mom died. Then I lost it. But, you're right. I bet she ain't too happy with me right now. I can do it." Now his voice trembled, "I love you man." He reached out and grabbed Chris's shoulder. They never were huggers.

"I love you like a brother." Chris pulled Willie to him and gave him a big bear hug with two slaps on the back while they both laughed at an old joke.

"Like a brother from another mother." Willie completed the joke, and they separated. "Guess I better get my ass in gear. Who made all this mess?"

Chris pulled a couple of twenty dollar bills out of his wallet. "Take a walk downtown later and get some food in this house. Make sure we have coffee. You know how I get if I don't have my coffee in the morning." With that, he turned and went out the back door. They both knew the money was a test, and both hoped it would be used for food.

Willie filled two garbage bags with all the newspapers, food wrappers, scraps, and empty bottles scattered on furniture and dropped on the floor throughout the house. He vacuumed and wiped down the kitchen counters, then started the first load of laundry. He thought his Mom would approve of his efforts, if not the end result. At least it was no longer, as she would have described it, a pig sty.

He picked up the money Chris had left, shoved it in his pants pocket and headed into town. He hadn't realized until he stepped outside what a beautiful day it was. The air was crisp, and the sky was so blue. As he approached Main Street he saw the line forming for lunch being served at the shelter. He looked at those lined up and realized what a sorry looking lot they were, and how close he had come to joining them. He had to pass by to get to the market, and thought about crossing the street to avoid contact, but stayed the course and started to head past, nodding to those he knew.

At the same time, Mrs. Mackenzie was coming down Main from the opposite direction and saw Willie, all cleaned up and walking with purpose. His posture revealed everything she needed to know. He had just about cleared past the entire group when Bud stepped out and stopped Willie's progress. Bud was a big guy, over six feet tall. He had been the star of the high school football team, and played varsity basketball and baseball. He had everything going for him. The high school girls were giddy over him. Teachers pumped up his grades, allowing him to keep his winning ways for their team. Everyone in town knew his name and cheered him on at every sporting event. But, his teachers hadn't done him any favors. He got a free ride to college, but dropped out after the second semester, unable to keep up his required grades. He couldn't hold down a job at any of the local businesses in town. He could barely read and write. He started a downward spiral that delivered him to where he was today.

Mrs. Mackenzie stepped into a doorway and watched the encounter in the reflection of the storefront display window.

"Where ya goin', Will? Church? Yer all cleaned up." Bud stumbled a couple of steps and smiled, revealing his stained teeth, two of which were missing. "What, ya gotta date?"

Willie just smiled back, realizing now that the other guys in line were turning to listen in on the conversation. "Hey, Bud. How you doin'? I'm just headed to Pat's Market up here. You gettin' some lunch?"

Bud pulled a paper bag with the head of a liquor bottle sticking out of the opening. "Got my lunch right here. Want a hit?" He leaned forward and reached out with his offering. His free hand travelled into his coat pocket and pulled out a clear plastic bag. "Or if you got a few bucks on you, I got something better here."

Mrs. Mackenzie held her breath as she saw Bud's offerings. She watched Willie slowly raise his right hand up toward the offerings. Her shoulders dropped. This was it. The guys in line all turned back to face forward. They all feared Bud. He used his size to intimidate, and they had no interest in taking part in another run-in with him.

"Not today, Bud." Willie said quietly as he pushed his palm straight out in front of him. "Not today." was all he could say. He turned to continue on to Pat's. Bud took a few seconds to interpret what had just happened while Willie took the time to put some distance between them. Bud yelled out some profanities behind him and then just kept calling out Willie's name. Willie didn't look back. He was in the next block when Mrs. Mackenzie stepped out of the doorway, acting as though she had just exited and wasn't aware of the drama that had just played out.

She smiled and said "Hello." Willie replied with a smile and a nod as he approached her, hoping Bud would lose interest in his mantra. Mrs. Mackenzie blocked his path, ever so slightly. "Aren't you Louise's son?" Willie stopped. "I used to sit next to her in church. She was a wonderful lady. She was very proud of you, you know. I was at her memorial service and wanted to tell you that, but never had the chance."

"You must mean my brother, Chris. He's in the National Guard." Willie smiled at this nice lady, mistaken as she was, wishing he could just get to the market without any further interruptions.

Before he could say anything further or start to move away, Mrs. Mackenzie took his arm and looked him straight in the eye, something he wasn't used to, especially from strangers. "No, she talked mostly about you, Willie. She said you were the best mechanic in the county. She said you never met an engine you couldn't fix. Aren't you the mechanic?"

"Well, I was. Yes. Kind of in between jobs right now." He started to look away and Mrs. Mackenzie tightened her grip, bringing him back to full attention.

"Why, you should head down to the Ford dealership. They have a sign in the window that says they are in need of a mechanic. I'm sure Mr. Hastings would love to have someone with your talents in his employ." Willie's gaze turned down Main Street toward the dealership. He decided not to give it too much thought, but to head right down and see if they were still looking for someone. He gently took Mrs. Mackenzie's hand from his arm and shook it in gratitude and farewell. "You tell Mr. Hastings that Mrs. Mackenzie sent you over. I buy all my cars there, so he owes me one." Willie was already headed in that direction and turned back to thank the woman, but she was gone. He glanced all around, but assumed she stepped back into the doorway she had been exiting, and headed on down to the Ford dealership. As he was approaching, he saw a man moving a large plant in the showroom window, and placing a handwritten sign in front of it. As he got closer, he saw the sign read "Wanted: Mechanic". He turned around one more time to see if Mrs. Mackenzie had reappeared, and then crossed the street to the dealership.

He hadn't been on too many job interviews, but this one seemed too easy. He introduced himself, asked for Mr. Hastings, using Mrs. Mackenzie's name, and started to tell of his experience with engines when he was interrupted with a question of when he could start. He was told what his wages and benefits would be, shook hands and was out the door just minutes after he had entered. He actually looked back up the street to where he had last seen Mrs. Mackenzie, but still, she was nowhere in sight. The line to the food pantry had moved into the building, so he had a clear path to the market and to return home. He couldn't wait to tell Chris.

When Bud approached the hot meal section of the kitchen with his tray, Mrs. Mackenzie looked up at him with a big spoonful of mashed potatoes ready to serve. He immediately looked down at his tray. "Hi Bud, how are you doing on this beautiful day? Looks like you've had a rough morning. You know we aren't supposed to serve anyone who is intoxicated. You aren't intoxicated, are you, Bud?' She held his serving back, waiting for his reply.

"Shut the fuck up and serve me my food, you old bitch. I don't need no sermons from you today." He was looking at Mrs. Mackenzie's neck, unwilling to raise his eyes up further.

"I'm not offering a sermon. I just asked you a question. But you certainly are in need of a sermon, young man." She shook the potatoes onto his plate and reached it out to him.

"Sorry, Miss Goody-Two-Shoes. Not today. I'm done with you and your stupid words. I'm not going to any more meetings with your "friends of God". They don't know what the fuck they're talking about. You can all go to Hell." He grabbed the plate from her and flung it right back in her direction. He was aiming for her head, but his throwing skills had diminished since high school and it sailed over her shoulder and into the pots hanging behind her. He turned to run, falling over an empty table and knocking over two chairs. He got up and ran to the door, turning over more chairs in his wake. Once outside, he ran up Main and turned down the alley to the dumpster he had laid claim to weeks ago. He sat against the pile of garbage that had not made it into the dumpster and caught his breath. He hated everyone and everything. He thought about the old woman at the food bank. She was relentless. Why couldn't she just leave him alone? He had had enough of her. He started thinking of ways to get her to stop interfering with him and his life. There was only one way. He looked around his immediate surroundings and spotted a long, sharp piece of metal that had been torn off the top of the dumpster, and next to it a brick. He thought about waiting for her to pass by his alley later that day to drag her back here and put an end to her meddling for good. It wouldn't be the first time he took care of someone in that way. He didn't need people looking down on him and pretending to care just to make themselves feel better. He began to tremble with his anxious thoughts. He decided he needed to calm himself down to carry out his plan. He reached into his coat pocket and pulled out the pills that Willie had turned down, thinking that maybe Willie would be next on his list. He washed the pills down with the remnants of the bottle in his brown paper bag and tossed it against the wall of the dumpster. He started to relax, and entered a familiar journey to a better, happier place. He closed his eyes, and stilled the waves of the ground rising and falling down the alleyway. He felt himself floating away, higher and higher. He opened his eyes and looked down. He saw himself lying there, trembling and writhing, then convulsing. Bud watched himself as his eyes rolled back in his head, and saw his hands approach his own throat, grasping for air. His fingernails dug in, scratching and clawing his neck and chest. Then, his body went limp. He continued to elevate, above the rooftops, above the city, and now up into a dark cloud. His journey on earth was over. He would have to start again, later, and learn what he hadn't in this lifetime, for this life had ended.

Before Chris left for Iraq, Jamie had a send-off party for his military brothers and invited his neighbors. He just had pizzas and grinders delivered, mostly because it was easy, but also remembering that when he was away from home, pizzas and grinders were one of the foods he missed most. Chris couldn't help but notice that Brent passed up a cold beer and reached for a Coke from the ice chest. He made his way over and asked quietly, "Not a fan of beer?"

"Eh, decided to give up drinking for a while. Didn't lead to anything good for me. Course, this Coke will probably keep me up all night." He smiled.

"Well, I have a brother, Willie, just quit the hard stuff. I'm afraid that while I'm gone he'll start hittin' it again. I'd feel a lot better if I knew there was someone back here, kinda lookin' out for him."

With all that Chris had done for Brent and Kim after the fire, Brent jumped at the chance to pay him back. It was the least he could do. "You got it, bro. Why don't we get together before you head out so I can meet him." They arranged to meet at the deli for lunch the next day, and shook on it. Chris felt that a huge weight was lifted from his chest.

Time moved forward. Missy was in a much better place. She kept busy with her new family of friends. She and Kathryn had become the best of friends, starting with their apple-picking excursions which resulted in more laughter than apples. She eventually left her job to work with Kathryn in her philanthropic endeavors.

Keith had left the grocery store chain once he and Kathryn were secure with the proceeds received from his first song. As promised, between the Drake brothers and the movie deal, they were more than comfortable with the income generated. He was able to spend more time with his music again, and wrote a few more songs that hit the charts. Kathryn was able to fulfill her dream of starting her own organization to help those in need. It kept her quite busy, but it was good busy. They were able to do some traveling and experience the world outside of their own.

Brent and Kim had a chance to get to know each other all over again. Kim started a support group in the basement of their chiropractic office for single parents dealing with cancer treatments. When she had been going through her own battle, she had spent chemo chair-time with a woman who had three sons at home, and confided that her biggest challenge was trying to keep up not only with the responsibilities of being a single parent, but shading her young sons from the fears of what she was going through. Kim's sister, of course, helped her with funding to assist members of her group that were in need. Brent had kept his promise to

Chris and kept in touch with Willie. While Chris was in Iraq, they went to a couple of baseball games to see the local team which was the minor league for the Chicago Whitesox. In their free time, Brent and Kim headed out of town on weekend getaways. They took up skiing in the winter months, and went hiking and kayaking during the summer. When they were home, they were happy to sit on the couch, share some popcorn and watch a good movie.

Jamie didn't stay long at The Commons. Shortly after his buddies were deployed, Missy, Brent and Kim came home to find notes on their doors saying goodbye and wishing them well. He left no forwarding information, but just said it was time to move on. They were all saddened by his departure, and hoped they might hear from him again once he got settled in to wherever he was headed. The apartment sat empty.

Willie kept his word to his brother, and had been sober now for over a year. He was a mechanic at the Ford dealership and when his brother Chris finished serving with the National Guard, Willie got him a job in sales. They shared the house they grew up in, built a large deck onto the back of the house, and revived the vegetable garden where their mother used to spend quiet hours planting, weeding and picking the fruits of summer. They expanded it to take up a good portion of the back yard. Willie teased Chris that this was a plan to reduce the size of the lawn which was Chris' responsibility to mow. Each Monday on their way to the dealership, they delivered their excess of veggies to the food bank, and Willie was grateful to be on the giving and not receiving end, thanks to his brother.

It was late in March when Mrs. Mackenzie decided to have the entire gang over for dinner. It was time. She contacted everyone and found a Friday night when they were all available and set the time for an early meal. Everyone was arriving from work, so they were happy to be invited to sit down to a good hot dinner together. The temperatures outside were frigid. It felt too cold even to snow, and the winds whipped down the streets as if they were racing against time.

The first to arrive were Willie and Chris. They parked Chris' truck across the street from The Commons and both noticed at the same time a figure sitting on the front steps. In the early darkness of winter they couldn't make out any features, but didn't think it was any of their crowd. They headed across the street and as they got closer, they saw the figure was a man. He looked like he might have gotten lost. Most of the street people and homeless hung out down off Main Street by the old factory building. They never ventured to this part of town. Without saying a word to each other, they each studied him from his toes up, mostly because his feet were the first to get their attention. He had no shoes. His socks were thread-thin and beyond dirty, with his big toe escaping from one of them. His pants were shabby to say the least, and too short to cover his lower legs which appeared pasty white and very thin. His massive hands hung over each knee with blackened fingernails. He had a heavy sweater which appeared much too big and a plaid scarf wrapped around his stubbly, wrinkled neck. His face was ruddy, with purple veins on each side of his nose. His eyes were bloodshot and cloudy. He had a baseball hat sitting backwards on his head. He didn't move as they approached, but just sat staring straight forward.

"Excuse me, sir, are you O.K.?" asked Chris as they stepped onto the sidewalk from the street. The man didn't reply. "Can I help you, sir? Are you, uh, lost?"

"Waiting for my daughter to come home." was the gravel throated reply. He smelled of urine and stale liquor.

"Who's your daughter?" asked Willie. The man's eyes shifted to Chris and Willie's feet.

"First floor. She'll be home at 6:30. Told me to wait here. What time is it?"

"It's 5:30, sir. Kind of cold to be sitting out here." Chris wasn't sure what to do. He didn't want to invite him to wait inside as he didn't know if there really was a daughter from the first floor coming home at 6:30. Still, the man didn't move. Willie looked at Chris, also wondering what they should do.

"I'm good. Spend everyday and every night in the cold. Don't worry. I'll be off your steps once she gets here."

Willie sat down on the steps next to the man and compared his boot to the man's foot, then untied his laces and pulled his boots off his feet. He kneeled in front of the man and slid each of his feet into the boots. He grasped the man's calves to hold his feet steady for the fitting, and tried not to cringe at the skin and bones he was encompassing with his own large hands. He laced and tied the boots, then raised back up and touched the man on his right shoulder. "You take care, sir."

The man didn't reply, or even move, as Chris and Willie continued up the stairs and into the building. As the door shut, headlights from Brent and Kim's car scanned past him while they turned into the parking area. They got out of their car and walked around the tree that once held the yellow plastic tape from their apartment fire. They were both startled when they realized there was a man sitting on their front steps. Other than his boots, he wasn't dressed well enough to be sitting outside. "Can I help you", asked Brent, directing Kim behind him with his right arm. The man didn't move.

"Waiting for the bus." His burst of a response encouraged a cough that sounded like it came from the earth below him, startling Kim to step back. There was a bus stop in front of their building, so his reply was believable. Brent took Kim's hand and headed up the stairs, staying to the far left, and entered the building, making sure the door shut securely behind them.

"Shouldn't we do something?" asked Kim as they headed to their apartment.

"I'm going to give him a blanket and one of my wool caps, but I wanted to get you inside. You never know." Brent went to the hall closet and removed a wool blanket and then plucked one of his wool caps from the coat rack by the door. He was back in less than a minute. "Hopefully, wherever he's headed, they won't steal his blanket."

Missy had been working with Kathryn all day on a project, so the two of them arrived with Keith and immediately spotted the same man, still sitting on the front steps of Missy's building. "Do you know that man?" Keith asked. Missy didn't recognize him from the building and Kathryn didn't recall ever seeing him at the shelter. As they approached him, Keith stepped forward to ask him the same questions as his friends had. In the meantime, Missy rushed past and up the stairs. Kathryn thought it a bit odd, but was concerned with the conversation her husband was attempting and turned all of her attention toward it.

Missy hurried with her keys and once inside went right to Steve's closet. She hadn't yet separated with all of his clothes, and knew exactly where his favorite winter coat still hung. She pulled it from the hanger and gave it a hug, smelling Steve's aftershave one last time before darting back out her door and out onto the front steps. Keith had offered to drive the visitor down to the shelter, while Kathryn called the man who was in charge to make sure they had a bed available. Kathryn was nodding yes to Keith, who reached out his hands to help the man up. As he stood, Missy wrapped Steve's coat around his shoulders, and gave him a pat. He was a little unsteady on his feet, so Keith put his arm around the man's waist and escorted him to his vehicle. As they drove off, Missy and Kathryn watched them make the turn, and then headed into the building without saying a word. They had become close friends, and words were not always necessary.

Keith returned about twenty minutes later and found everyone in Mrs. Mackenzie's apartment. They had already discussed the man on the stairs, so Keith just said that he would be taken care of tonight, at least, and the conversation soon turned to each other, as they hadn't all been together in a while. In the kitchen, Mrs. Mackenzie was smiling and singing a tune to herself. If they only knew who had just visited the building, and what had just taken place. If they only knew.

As always, everyone had a grand time together with good food, and much laughter. Two by two they departed when the evening was getting on until only Missy was left, helping Mrs. Mackenzie to clear the table and rinsing the dishes to load into the dishwasher. Missy had no idea that this would be the last time she would see the woman she had come to know as "Mrs. Mackenzie".

Mrs. Mackenzie wished with all of her heart that she could tell Missy how they all came to be together. She wished she could tell her that she had been Miss Crawford, the pretty faced second grade teacher at Union Elementary School who had died from pneumonia after suffering a long illness. Her best years of teaching had been with Kim and Kathryn in her class, along with Chris' mom, Louise, a few years prior, sitting next to Steve, who later became Missy's love of her life. She wished she could explain to her that Mr. Crawford from next door had been her brother, and that his spirit was now alive and well. Mostly, she wished she could tell Missy that Steve and Jason were watching over her, and patiently waiting for her to live out her life and join them someday. Mrs. Mackenzie wished she could tell Missy everything, but even she wasn't privileged to know everything. She knew it was her mission to keep those she loved and cared about safe from Evil, and for them to learn their life lessons, to be the best they could be. But, she knew Missy wasn't ready to know all of that yet. Missy still had reason to stay and carry out her own mission in this lifetime, and what a beautiful life she was going to have. Miss Crawford, aka "Mrs. Mackenzie" had fulfilled her destiny, and her brother had joined her, up above. She could now move on, leaving her students to their own angels who would watch over them for as long as was needed, until they would join the glory that awaited all good souls.

CHAPTER TWO

Back at the Farm

As the bus pulled into the station, Jamie used the seat in front of him to pull himself up, hesitating to allow his hip to engage his leg. He was stiff from the long ride. He pulled his backpack from the rack overhead and headed for the door. The aisle was narrow, exaggerating his usual awkward gate. He stepped off the bus and headed into the terminal. There was no one to greet him. No one knew he was there. He passed through the building and out the front door, hoping to see a line of cabs looking for passengers. No cabs. He started walking toward the center of town, where the statue of a pioneer settler with a rifle in one hand and a shovel in the other would point the way home. He grew up in this town and knew every square inch of it, but as he looked around, Jamie realized he no longer knew any of its inhabitants, except for the statue. The pioneer was looking to the west, and Jaime turned at First Avenue to walk two more blocks before he was out of town. From here he turned onto County Road 29, and began the four mile walk to the family farm. It was warm for early April, and he was glad for it, as his New Balance sneaker wouldn't have served him well if there had been any snow on the ground. He unzipped his fleece so he wouldn't get overheated, keeping up a steady march along the roadside. He hadn't called his parents to tell them he would be coming. He wanted to surprise them. His father's birthday was coming up, and he was turning 60. Jamie figured most of the family would head home for the celebration, and looked forward to spending some time with them. He hadn't seen some of his aunts and uncles since before he joined the guard, and he wanted them to see that he had changed his ways. A few cars sped by as he continued on, and then a police car passed him and slowed to a stop. It sat with its brake lights lit until he got close enough to see the driver's eyes watching him in the rear view mirror. The brake lights dimmed as the officer put the car in park, and opened his door. Jamie stopped walking and watched as the officer stood up and turned around. Jamie's heart stopped.

"You Ed and Mary Reed's son?" called out the officer, looking stern and in need of an eyebrow trim.

"Yes, sir." Jamie dared to move a muscle.

"Saw that on the label of your pack there." Jamie still used the digital camouflage backpack issued to him, which bared his last name. It was the reason most of his buddies called him Reed, though they knew it wasn't really his first name.

He continued to stand as still as the statue in town, unable to read the police officer's expression. He had left town with a bad reputation, and didn't blame anyone for relying on this reflection.

"Heard you had a rough go of it over there. I thank you for your service and for your sacrifice, young man. Your parents know you're coming home?"

Jamie was starting to relax, but just answered the question, "No, sir."

"Well, climb in. I'll give you a ride."

Jamie walked to the car and started to open the back door.

"Oh no, you sit in front, boy."

Jamie maneuvered his back pack from his shoulders and followed orders. As he buckled in, the officer looked over and extended a large hand. "I'm Kyle. Kyle Morrison."

"Yes, sir. I'm Jamie. Appreciate the ride."

As Kyle put the car in gear, he turned on the siren and lights. Then the officer hit the gas peddle so hard Jamie's head jerked back and hit the headrest. "They're gonna hear you comin' now. Givin' you a hero's welcome, Jamie."

They sped down the road, and arrived at the farm entrance in a matter of minutes, pulling into the driveway with gravel flying. Jamie saw the fence rail posts speed past in a blur. As they rounded the bend by the milking barn he got a full view of his house. His sister was out on the front porch, holding the door open. As Kyle hit the brakes, the car turned sideways, so Jamie could make a grand exit from the car and up the cobblestoned walkway. As he opened the car door he saw his mother standing behind his sister, peering over her shoulder. Thankfully, his lead-footed chauffeur turned the siren off, but the lights continued to circle. Jamie turned out and lifted his leg out onto the driveway gravel. As he lifted himself out of the vehicle, he saw his father marching from the milking barn to see what the ruckus was about. His father's eyes fixed on Kyle. Jamie looked back to see a big smile on Kyle's face, which eased the initial fears of Jamie's father. He ran to his son, grabbed his shoulders to give him a proud eye-to-eye look, and hugged him, hard. By now his sister and mother reached him, still standing at the door of the cruiser. His mother, crying hugged him, then held his face in her rough hands, taking him in before making an entrance for his sister. As his sister pulled away from their embrace she turned her head, looking away, but he immediately noticed that make-up wasn't fully covering a bruise under her left eye. As she pulled her arms back from the hug, he saw that her sweater sleeves had gotten rolled up as she attempted to quickly pull them back to cover her arms, which were also bruised. Her eyes flashed up to see if her brother had seen them. She gave a slight "no" shake, signaling him to keep quiet. Jamie obeyed.

"So good to see you, son. You look great." his father choked the words out. His mother had pulled a laced handkerchief from her vest pocket and dried her tears.

"Good to be home, sir."

Kyle came around with Jamie's backpack and said he'd be on his way. As he turned the car to leave, the family headed to the house. Jamie couldn't help but notice the place looked a little dim. The house needed a good coat of paint, and some repairs. Some fence rails were broken by the barn, and the shed's door was askew. Once inside the house, everything looked just as his memory said it should. "Something smells good."

Jamie's sister headed for the kitchen saying, "Mom's got one of your favorite dinners in the oven, pot roast and sweet potatoes."

"If you want to wash up, supper should be ready, and we can catch up at the table." his mother took his face one more time in her hands, then continued to the kitchen. Jamie was home, and he couldn't think of anywhere else he would rather be.

"So, how are things with the farm, Dad?" Jamie was always more comfortable asking questions than answering them. He immediately noticed his sister's head notch down.

The family took their seats at the kitchen table. Jamie's father, Ed, forked a piece of meat and placed it on his plate. "Tough, son, tough. Milk prices go up, but the suppliers and grocery chains don't pass it on to us farmers. At the same time, we pay higher prices for our corn seed, and fuel. Makes it tough. I've had to let go of a couple of milkers been with me for years, and still can't make ends meet. I don't know where the money goes. I keep askin' your sister how I can be working harder than ever, and making less and less."

"I can stick around for a while, and help you out. Looks like you could use a few repairs, and I'm sure I haven't forgotten how to milk a cow." Jamie smiled at his dad, but his dad didn't look up from his plate. Jaime turned to his sister. "How's the boy, Cindy? He must be getting big."

Jamie's sister reached for her water glass, "Tommy's taller than me now, almost six feet. I have to look up at him to tell him to clean his room. He's good. I can't wait to tell him you're home. He'll be so excited to see you."

"And Vick?" Jamie never cared for his brother-in-law, but he put out the gesture for his sister's sake. She finished drinking her water and wiped nothing from her mouth with her napkin.

"He's good. Still driving for Allied. He's doing shorter runs now, though. So he's home more often." Cindy still didn't make eye contact with her brother, but refilled her glass from the pitcher on the table and topped off her father's glass. She was afraid her brother would ask her about the bruises, though she had quickly refreshed the makeup below her eye before they sat down at the table.

Jamie turned his attention to his mother. "So, any party plans for Dad's 60th?"

His mother smiled and glanced at Jamie's father. "Your father says he doesn't want a party, but he's having one. I've got all the relatives coming. We're going to have it here, and everyone is bringing a dish. We'll plan to have it out back, but if the weather looks bad, we'll move it into the barn. The Thompson boys said their band will play for free, and the Carters from the next farm over are going to roast one of their pigs." She paused and looked at her son. "I'm so glad you'll be here for the celebration."

"Sounds great, Mom. Will Uncle Gus be here in time?" Jamie's favorite uncle growing up was actually his father's cousin. Gus lived in Alaska, but would travel down to the farm in his trailer each summer and spend a month, helping out. He used to take Jamie to the lake on Sunday afternoons, rain or shine, and they would fish from the canoe he stored behind the garage. Uncle Gus told the best stories about living in Alaska. Jamie loved to hear about his hunting adventures, and it was his uncle that taught him to shoot, which was a great advantage to Jamie when he entered the Guard.

Everyone at the table stopped eating and looked at Jamie. He got a bad feeling from the expression on their faces. His father spoke. "August is gone, Jamie. We got word just before you left for basic training. He had passed a couple of months before, but it took them a while to find out who his family was down here. I decided not to tell you then, to let you keep your mind on what you were about to do. Then you were heading out to Iraq, and I figured I might as well wait until you got back. Then you got hurt and..." His father's voice cracked as he looked away from his son.

Jamie felt a heaviness in his chest. He understood why they hadn't shared the bad news earlier. It wouldn't have served a purpose. And now, he suddenly recalled seeing his Uncle Gus as he rose above his body in that helicopter just after he was blown off his feet by the IED. It all made sense now. But, he also recalled that during some tough times over there he would picture himself after returning home with Gus, in that canoe, fishing poles in hand, waiting for a bite. Only in his mind, this time, Jamie could be telling the tales, and maybe impress his Uncle Gus with the brave man he had become.

He reached for his father's hand and covered it with his own. "I understand, Dad. Thanks."

There was a brief silence. Everyone had emptied their plates, some more than once, so Cindy suggested the men move into the living room while the women did the dishes.

"No. Mom, why don't you and Dad go relax out on the front porch and I'll clean up with Cindy. Like old times, but this time we won't fight. Promise." Jamie stood, picked up his plate, and headed for the sink. Jamie's father looked at his mother.

"Come on, Mary. Haven't sat with you on the porch swing in a long time." Jamie turned back to see his father take his mother's hand. It looked like she was blushing.

"I can handle these, Jamie. Go join them." Cindy nodded in the direction of her parents. She wanted to avoid alone time with Jamie.

Jamie pulled the dishpan from under the sink and turned the hot water on. "Nope. I'm washin' and you're dryin'." Once he heard the screen door leading out to the front porch bang shut, he continued. "And, talkin'."

Cindy carried the silverware she had collected and dropped them in the dishpan. "What?" She tried to act nonchalant.

"What's with the bruises, Cindy?"

She took the dish towel off the hook on the wall above the sink. "Nothing you have to worry about, Jamie."

"Might as well tell me, cause we aren't leaving this kitchen 'til you do."

"I can handle things. I don't want you to get involved. It'll make it worse. Really, just, just don't worry about it."

"Tell me."

Cindy shook her head. "Vick just got carried away one night. He didn't mean it. He was mad, and I locked myself in the bathroom. By the time he got the door off the hinges, he was out of control. I shouldn't have locked the door. It was my fault." Her voice had trailed down to a whisper.

"Was Tommy home?"

Cindy's shoulders slumped. "Yes, but I don't think he heard anything. He goes to sleep with those headphones on. I really don't think he heard anything. Didn't seem like it the next morning. Please, promise me you won't get involved, Jamie. Vick has been better since it happened. I think he scared himself, strange enough. Mom and Dad haven't noticed. Dad would explode. He has enough to worry about. Just let it be. Please, for me."

Jamie didn't commit to her request. He knew Vick was scum the first time they met. His sister's story didn't surprise him at all. Jamie's time in the Guard had connected him with real men with real values. Vick was all bravado, driving a big rig made him think he was a big man. But, he was as small as they come. He had always been abusive to Cindy, verbally. He ordered her around like she was his dog. Jamie never understood what she saw in such a runt of a man.

They finished the dishes in silence, and then Cindy went out on the porch and told her mother she better get going. Vick was on the road, but Tommy would be home soon, and she wanted to be there when he arrived. She had packaged up a plate to warm up for his dinner. She gave Jamie a hug before heading to her car.

As she drove away, their father said, "Girl has lost her spirit." Jamie and his parents sat out on the porch, listening to the sounds of the night emerging.

"I'm going to head up to bed. Coming, Ed?"

"Yes, dear. Morning will be here before you know it. Stay up as long as you want, son. I'm sure you can find your room. it's just as you left it." Ed got up off the swing to follow his wife." Glad you're home, son. Glad you're home."

Mary stopped on her way in the house, kissed Jamie on the top of his head, and patted his cheek, smiling sweetly. His parents went inside. It had been a long day for Jamie, but he sat out on the porch for a while, content to be home, but thinking about his sister, his Uncle Gus, and how hard his father was working for such little reward. Eventually, his eyes told him it was time to go to sleep, so he headed up to his old room. It was just as he had left it.

He awoke to a sound he wasn't sure of. It was somewhere between a thud and a bang. Was it a door shutting? Jamie looked around in the dark, and for a few seconds, wasn't sure where he was. There was a bit of moonlight coming in through the opened curtains of a window. He turned his head and saw the dark shadow of a figure standing over his bed. Beyond the figure, light was coming in through the doorway, indicating he was home, in his own room. That settled, he squinted, trying to make out the figure over him. It was a man, too big to be his father. The figure moved a bit to the side, and the light from the window shined on the face. "Uncle Gus!" Jamie called out, sitting upright and reaching out. The image straightened upright, and disappeared. Jamie blinked, and looked around the darkness of his room. He sat, leaning against his headboard, trying to see any trace of his visitor again. He closed his eyes and reopened them, staring into the night. The moment was gone. He eventually slid back down and pushed his pillow under his head. Sleep did not return for a long time. He again thought about his family, and what he could do to help.

The smell of bacon and coffee woke him from a sound sleep. He opened his eyes and immediately recalled the events of the night, searching his room for any evidence of his uncle. He decided to keep the experience to himself, using the excuse that it was probably just a dream. But he knew it wasn't.

Jamie reached for his prosthetic and began his daily routine of getting hooked up and using the rest of his body to swing himself out of bed, then standing to test himself and make sure everything was correct before he engaged himself to walk. He pulled some clean jeans and a t-shirt from the shelves in his closet and got dressed.

When he arrived downstairs, his mother was just putting breakfast on the table as his father came in through the kitchen door, heading to the sink to wash up. He had already finished with the first milking of the day.

"How do you make breakfast smell so good, Mary? That bacon has been calling me in here from the barn." Ed kissed his aproned wife on the cheek, then greeted his son, "Mornin'. How did ya sleep, son?"

"With my eyes closed." Jamie punch-lined an old family joke. As the men took their seats at the kitchen table, he asked, "I'm all yours today, Dad. Got any projects for me?"

"Too many to name. Figure you can still run a tractor, with your leg and all?" Jamie's mother shot a look at her husband. "Just askin' is all, Mary."

"Guess we'll find out. I'm pretty sure I can still shift, no problem asking." Jamie pulled his mother's chair out for her to join them.

"Just don't you push yourself to do anything you're not comfortable doing. You don't have to prove anything to us, that's for sure." Mary nodded to her son, then poured them all a cup of coffee.

When they finished breakfast, Mary headed for the sink while Ed headed upstairs to shower. He always waited until after the first milking so as not to wake his wife when he got up at 4:00 a.m.

Jamie circled through the living room and dining room, glancing at the old pictures of family on the walls. He passed by the office where he recalled playing with his race cars on the floor while his father worked at the desk for what seemed like hours. He entered and saw the old adding machine. No computers here, everything was still done on paper. He saw an opened bank statement that Cindy must have been working on when he arrived the day before. He noticed some cancelled checks, payable to "Cash". Jamie was curious what this would be about and turned the checks over. They were all endorsed by his sister. Part of him felt he should stop snooping, but another part opened the checkbook to see if there was an explanation written in the check register. The register wasn't agreeing with the checks, according to the numbers. Each check cashed by Cindy was showing in the register as being payable to the gas company, the feed store, and other suppliers that Jamie recognized by name. He started to get a sick feeling about what he was seeing, and sat down at the desk, hoping he would discover that he was wrong. He found previous bank statements in one of the desk drawers, and saw the same practices with checks. Could this be why his father was having trouble making ends meet? Could his sister really be stealing from her own family business? He left the office and shut the door behind him, as though this gesture might make his findings go away.

Jamie heard his father heading down the stairs and joined him in the hallway, hoping his father wouldn't notice his discern. "Ready to get some shit done, son?" Ed asked, hooking his arm around his son's neck.

Jamie had a feeling from his father's smile what was in store. Since there was no snow on the ground, the time was ripe to spread cow manure in the fields so it would have time to break down before they planted the corn in the spring. Jamie backed the tractor up to the spreader and drove over to the vats of manure. As he passed his father, he got a thumbs up.

They worked all morning, then headed back to the house for lunch.

"Cindy a no-show again?" Ed asked Mary.

Jamie's mother placed sandwiches in front of each of them without making eye contact. "She had some errands to do today."

Jamie's father confided in Jamie. "She only shows up one or two days a week anymore. Not sure what's going on, but something is up with your sister. When she is here, it seems like she is somewhere else. Can't talk to her about anything; she'll just up and leave. Maybe you can figure her out."

It crossed Jamie's mind to reveal to his father what he had seen in the office, but decided it would be better if he asked Cindy about it first. He didn't want to show up and start troubles in the family, although it seemed trouble showed up before he did. "Seen Vick at all?" was the safest comeback he had.

"Can't tell you the last time he was here. She makes excuses for him at holidays. Just she and Tommy were here at Christmas. When I asked her if Vick was on the road, she said he was home and would come by later in the day. Never did." Ed sipped his coffee and took a giant bite off his sandwich. They ate in silence, then Ed went out to check the mailbox.

Jamie cleared the table and asked his mother, "Cindy confide any troubles to you?"

Mary shook her head and said, "No. When I ask too many questions she shuts down, so I let her be. She'll talk when she's ready. Just hope Tommy doesn't see it like we do. A boy should have a solid home. It's hard enough growing up." She folded the dishtowel on its hook and smoothed her apron, then looked her son square in his eyes. "Glad to see how you turned out. You're a good man. You handled your injuries better than anyone I know would have done. Shows how strong you are inside. I hope you know how much your father and I love you." At this point her voice cracked and she had to look away. Jamie hugged his mother and whispered in her ear.

"I love you too." They heard the bang of the screen door and parted before Ed came back into the kitchen.

"Nothing but bills in the mail today. Sorry I went and fetched it. Ready to get back to work, son?"

Father and son worked through the afternoon. Jamie's hours on the tractor gave him time to think further about his sister, and how he should approach helping her, without turning her away. Vick had bullied her for so long, and Jamie wanted her to get some self-esteem back, and to know she deserved better. He realized he needed to know more about the cashed checks, and how Tommy was doing before he took any action.

When Jamie finished fertilizing the lower field, he headed back to the barn. It was getting late in the day, and his father was probably just finishing up with the afternoon milking. As he lowered the front bucket and turned the tractor off, he heard a car pulling into the yard. He recognized Cindy's car from the previous night, and noticed she had a passenger. It looked like Vick, but there was no way in hell he would ever let her drive him anywhere. Jamie had come up with a pretty good system to exit the tractor, using his upper body to hold on as he backed off the side, squaring up and settling his weight on the ground below. As he turned around, he saw that it was indeed not Vick with Cindy, but Tommy, who was standing half way between the car and his Uncle Jamie. It was the first time Tommy had seen him since he lost his leg. While his jeans covered his prosthetic, Tommy took a second to settle himself from the view of Jamie's robotic departure from the tractor. At the same time, Jamie took his time to take in the young man that Tommy had become. He was tall and strong, looking too much like Vick did the first time Jamie laid eyes on him. Their assessments finished, Tommy's face broke into a huge smile, and his likeness to his father vanished. He ran to Jamie and put his arms out half way there, alerting Jamie to follow suit, as a big man hug was coming, full steam. They finalized their hug with two back slaps to indicate it was time to separate, as men do, and Tommy backed away, looking straight into his uncle's eyes. "It's so awesome to see you, Uncle Jamie. You look great."

"Dude, when did you become a man? What the hell has your mom been feeding you? Look at you. Jesus." Jamie reached back to steady himself against the tractor. Looking up at his nephew had taken him a bit off balance. "So, what are you, now? Twenty, thirty?"

Tommy smirked at Jamie. "I'll be seventeen in two months. Mom keeps promising me she's gonna start letting me drive." Tommy had turned up his volume on the last sentence, so his approaching mother would get one more hint.

"Be plenty of time for that, son. Don't worry." Cindy looked past her brother to the lower field. "Wow, you got it all spread? That should make Dad happy. I know he's been wanting to get it done."

Ed approached his family and fixed his eyes on his grandson. "Tommy, did you grow some since last week?". He turned to Jamie and boasted, "Can you believe this boy?"

Tommy looked down at the ground and shook his head at the attention he was getting, then looked up at his uncle. "How long you stayin'?" It was a question no one had yet asked, but everyone had wondered.

"Hope to be here a while...long as they'll have me, I guess." Jamie received another big smile from his nephew.

Cindy nudged her son. "O.K., you got to see your uncle, but we gotta get going. Your father is supposed to be home for dinner tonight, and I have to get it started." As they turned to depart, Tommy looked one more time at Jamie. "Maybe I could come over this weekend and we could, like, hang out."

"For sure, man."

As Cindy turned the car around to leave, Tommy waived goodbye to the two men who were heading to the house.

The next morning Jamie awoke to the sound of voices coming from the kitchen downstairs. He couldn't make out what was being said, but it sounded like his father and Cindy were at odds.

By the time he climbed out of bed and assembled himself, the discussion had ended. He washed up, got dressed and headed down. Ed was sitting at the kitchen table eating a bowl of cereal and reading the newspaper. Jamie poured himself a cup of coffee and sat down across from his father. "Mornin' Dad."

"Yes it is."

Jamie looked around, then asked, "Did I hear Cindy down here?"

"She's in the office." Ed continued to stare at the paper, turning the pages and glancing at headlines. Eventually, he finished, got up from the table, and headed for the shower. Jamie took the opportunity to talk to Cindy. He stood in the doorway of the office, knowing his sister had to have heard his approach in the hallway.

"Morning. You're here bright and early." No response. "Where's Mom?"

"She went to the grocery store. She took my car. Hers didn't have gas." As Cindy glanced up quickly at Jamie, he thought he noticed the right side of her chin looked red, and puffed out. He stepped in to get a better view, sitting in the old worn-leather chair across the desk from her. He saw the stack of bank statements he had pulled from the drawer the morning before, and realized he had left everything out on the desk. She was assembling the checks and statements back into their envelopes, appearing a bit flustered as she did so. Jamie decided this wasn't the time to confront her, so he got back up from the chair to leave the office. Cindy didn't look up, but said, "Tommy asked if I would bring him over tomorrow so he could spend time with you. Is that O.K.?"

Jamie stopped at the door. "Yah, I'd like that. Doesn't he have school?"

"Tomorrow's Saturday."

"Oh yah, I guess it is. O.K., yah. See you later."

Jamie headed out to the barn to fuel up the tractor. He was so anxious to have a good talk with Cindy, but knew he had to pick the right time as it was probably going to be a one shot deal. As he finished up he saw his father headed his way. He moved the empty fuel jug to the side of the garage and saw his uncle's old wooden canoe resting on its side with grass and weeds almost covering it from view. He immediately knew what he and Tommy would be doing the next day. He thought it strange that one of the weeds he recognized in the camouflage of growth was one Uncle Gus used to call "bittersweet".

Mary outdid herself at breakfast on Saturday morning. When she heard Tommy was coming she started up the grill for hotcakes and bacon. Jamie was amazed at the amount of food his nephew could consume. When the clicking of forks on dishes slowed to a pace that indicated the feeding frenzy was coming to an end, Mary sat down to enjoy her own breakfast. Jamie was impressed when Tommy got up from the table to carry his dishes to the sink and thanked his grandmother.

Jamie had spent some time the night before assembling his meager stash of fishing equipment, and had it waiting out on the back step. As they headed outside he asked Tommy, "Like to fish?" He grabbed his old spinning rods and nodded down for Tommy to pick up the tackle box. Tommy looked down at the box, covered in stickers from Jamie's childhood, and held shut by a large rubber band.

"Cool." was Tommy's reply. Then he asked, "Do we have a boat?"

"This way." Jamie nodded toward the garage and started off in that direction. He looked back to see Tommy scanning the garage and surrounding area looking for a boat. When they arrived at the canoe Jamie stopped. "Here she is." Tommy continued to look around and then gave his uncle a look.

"Where?"

Jamie gave the buried canoe a thump with the butt of one of his fishing rods, and Tommy looked down, slowly recognizing bits and pieces of the exposed canoe underbelly through the growth of yellowed weeds.

"Cool. Is this yours?"

"It belonged to my uncle, my Uncle Gus. I'm sure he would be happy to see us use it. Let's get her out of this brush and turn her over."

Tommy quickly set the tackle box down and stepped to what looked like the middle of the canoe, grabbing the side that leaned against the shed. The weeds had been weakened by winter, and gave up the canoe they had held captive without a fight. He turned it over and they set their equipment inside. Tommy grabbed the strap attached to the front of the canoe and started off dragging it in the direction of the lake.

It was a great day. Tommy spoke easily to his uncle, telling him all about school, his friends, his favorite sports teams and the latest gossip from town. He was able to get Jamie to share a few stories from Iraq, but Jamie tried to keep them on the lighter side in keeping with the spirit of the day. The water was still a bit cold for the fish to be out and about, but they did manage to get a few bites. The sun danced on the water and eventually moved overhead, indicating that the morning was coming to an end, so they reeled in their lines and headed back to the farm. They spent the afternoon tinkering with some of the farm equipment that was in need.

Jamie was surprised at Tommy's knowledge of mechanics and such. He seemed to anticipate his uncle's next move and had a tool ready or was right there to lift something heavy out of the way, without making Jamie feel handicapped. Cindy pulled in and beeped her horn, indicating that it was time for Tommy to leave, as she stayed behind the wheel. Tommy wiped his hand on his pant leg and reached it out to shake his uncle's hand. Jamie obliged, pulling Tommy toward him and placed his other hand on the boy's shoulder and said "Thanks. I had a great day."

"No, I had a great day. Thanks, Uncle Jamie." The car horn beeped again and Tommy ran to the vehicle. When he opened the car door he seemed to step back a bit and stiffen up, then slowly got into car and pulled the door shut. As the car pulled away Jamie watched, waiting to receive a goodbye wave.

He was used to seeing bruises on his mother, usually covered with makeup, but this was the worst. Her eye was swollen shut and she had a cut on her lip. They drove home in silence. As she shifted into park and turned the key she instructed Tommy. "Just go in the house and head up to your room. He's in a bad way today. Don't make no never mind to anything he says. You stay in your room and I'll bring you something to eat later."

They walked in the front door and Vick was sitting in his chair. He had a baseball bat across his lap, and a pile of balls on his side table. For a split second, Tommy thought he was looking to go outside and hit a few balls, but then he realized from his father's stare how ridiculous that idea was. Cindy put her hand on her son's back and gave him a slight push toward the stairs to his room, but Tommy was frozen. His father stood up and palmed one of the baseballs, staring at him during the process. "Welcome home, son. Did you have a fun day with your uncle gimpy? Big war hero. Zero to hero. Tell me what you did with your new friend. Did you play hopscotch?" Vick followed the question with a sick smile. "Answer me goddammit!"

Tommy couldn't breathe. When he spoke, he didn't recognize his own voice. He squeaked his reply, "We went fishing and stuff." Vick tossed the ball straight up and swung the bat, connecting the two. The ball flew past Tommy's head and hit the door frame behind him.

"What did ya talk about, Tommy?"

As Vick picked up another ball, Tommy tried to step back, but his mother was standing behind

him, quaking. "Just stuff, school and stuff."
Another ball was struck in Tommy's direction,
hitting his shoulder. He flinched, but didn't
move.

"Did you tell him bout me? Tell him I lost my job
last year? I bet you had a lot to talk about."
Now he gripped the bat and started to walk
toward Tommy. He reached back to try to move
his mother back out the door, but she was
frozen. He was trapped between them. His
father started swinging the bat, knocking over
the lamp next to the couch. Tommy turned to
look as the lamp smashed to the floor, taking his
eyes off his father who took the advantage and
swung the bat hard, hitting Tommy's upper arm
and knocking him off balance. As he took a
couple of steps to regain his stance, Cindy was
left exposed. Vick tried to quickly swing the bat
again, but missed her with an awkward attempt,
which added to his rage. Tommy moved quickly
to the middle of the room to distract his father
away from her. He could see his father trying to
decide on his next target, so he picked up a
stack of magazines from the table, which helped
his father to make a decision, turning his
attention to Tommy. This gave Cindy a chance
and she took it, running out of the door. Tommy
heard the car engine start and roar away as his
father stepped closer to him, raising the bat. He
swung hard, but Tommy raised the magazines,
holding them in front of his head. His hand took
the brunt of the blow, and the magazines
sprawled to the floor. He jumped over the couch
and Vick made a move to follow, but slipped on
the magazines. At the same time he hit his head

on the coffee table, he lost his grip on the bat, giving himself a slight blow to his own head. Tommy ran into the kitchen and pulled a carving knife from the block. He heard his father groaning and thumping his way back up to his feet. Tommy stood staring at the kitchen door, holding the knife in his uninjured hand. Time stood still. He considered crossing the kitchen to look through the door. Maybe his father had knocked himself out. He listened to the silence, hoping for an indication of his father's location, but it was dead quiet. He tried to catch his breath with slow steady inhales. He was sure his father was in the other room, also listening with intent. Tommy felt his heart beating out of his chest, and feared his heart and lungs were giving him away. Minutes passed. He didn't move a muscle, staring at the empty doorway, barely blinking. He decided to change his grip on the knife. As he loosened his fingers to do so, the knife slipped from the sweat of his palm and fell to the floor. As he hurried to pick it up his father charged through the doorway and swung the bat with both hands, hitting Tommy squarely on the back of his head. As his face smashed down on the kitchen floor he heard a loud crash and caught a glimpse of Vick falling down next to him. He heard a man yell. "What the fuck are you doing?" He knew the voice, but wasn't sure. Then he heard his mother scream. He couldn't move, but looked at his father, lying nearby, and saw his hand reaching toward him, then grasping the knife that was still at Tommy's side. Vick curled his fingers around the handle and slid the knife under him.

"Is he dead?" Tommy heard his mother ask.

A hand reached down to Vick's shoulder to turn him over. As he was being turned, he stabbed his new victim fiercely, and Tommy saw his Uncle Jamie fall down to the kitchen floor between them. He saw his uncle's eyes wide open, and staring straight ahead. Then he heard his mother's grunt, as she slammed her husband's head with his own bat, knocking him back down on top of Jamie.

Jamie looked down, through a haze of white, and saw the pile of bodies. His brother-in-law was covering most of himself, and his nephew laid next to him, twitching, a pool of blood by his head. He watched from above, as his sister stood over her husband, bat paused and ready to swing again if needed. He had been here before, watching over himself. This time he wasn't in a helicopter, but in his sister's kitchen. He felt a hand on his shoulder. It was a hand of reassurance, and didn't alarm him. He continued to stare down at himself, but somehow knew who was with him. He reached a hand across his chest and rested it on the comforting hand. They did not speak with words, but seemed to read each other's thoughts.

"Here you are, again."

"Where is here?"

"Here is where you are supposed to be. You are always where you are supposed to be."

"I don't understand."

"No, you don't. You can't understand, and I can't explain it. But, just know you have always been where you were meant to be, and you always chose the right path. Think about this. You have more to do. It is not your time. But I am so proud of the man you are. Your soul is rich."

"Will I see you again?" Jamie felt himself being pulled back down to where his physical body rested.

"Not for a while, but I am always with you."

"Wait, Uncle Gus...." but it was too late. Jamie was back on the kitchen floor. He heard sirens in the distance, growing louder. Then all went black.

Cindy stood over Vick, the bat still raised over her head. Her focus, however, rested on her son. Tommy hadn't moved. She looked at the small pool of blood near his head then stared at his back, looking for evidence that he was still breathing. She didn't notice that Jamie had slid his hand out from underneath him, and palmed the floor to slowly pull himself out from underneath Vick. He moved as slowly as he could, trying not to alert Vick, if he was still alive. As Jamie cleared Vick's weight he rolled onto his right side, facing Vick. Vick's left hand firmed its grip on the handle of the bloodied knife, out of Jamie's view. Cindy was still fixated on her son, and everything else in the room was a blur. Like

93

a bolt of lightening, Vick raised himself up and aimed the knife at Jamie's exposed chest. With a guttural roar, he started a downward lunge of the knife. Suddenly, there was a loud explosion in the room and Vick's chest purged blood as he collapsed. Jamie turned his head to the doorway, where Officer Kyle Morrison stood, pistol still positioned to shoot again if necessary.

Jamie reached over and put two fingers on the side of Vick's neck, than shook his head up and down, looking back at Kyle. "He's done." Kyle reached for the bat and removed it from Cindy's hands, as she lowered them to her sides, still staring at Tommy, who moved a leg and groaned. The scream of an ambulance siren increased and then wound down, indicating its arrival. The room filled with medics, firefighters and police. Tommy and Jamie were loaded onto stretchers and into the ambulances, with Cindy by Tommy's side. Vick's body was covered with a blanket.

Kyle sat at the kitchen table, reporting to his Sargent that he received a call from Ed Reed saying that his daughter had just come to the house in a panic that Vick was beating up on Tommy with a bat, and she had just left with her brother. Kyle detailed that he arrived at Cindy & Vick's house and saw the front door was open. He entered and saw that they were all in the kitchen. He drew his weapon and stepped from behind Cindy just as Vick attempted to stab Jamie in the chest. He shot once, and it was fatal. The police followed through with photos, and samples of fingerprints, blood samples, and reports. A cruiser was sent to pick up Ed and Mary to join their family at the hospital.

Uncle Gus looked down upon Jamie and smiled.

CHAPTER THREE

After School

Claire looked at the clock on the nightstand. "Tommy, you gotta get up. Aren't they supposed to be here at 10:00?" She nudged her boyfriend repeatedly until he groaned.

"Stop. What time is it?" he asked, looking at the clock for himself. "Holy shit. We gotta get up. You gotta go. I gotta get in the shower and get dressed. They're supposed to be here at 10:00!"

Claire climbed out of bed with Tommy right behind and reached for her jeans draped on the chair. "O.K., I'll see you at graduation."

Tommy slammed the bathroom door behind him, then re-opened it and grinned at her. "See you at graduation."

Claire straightened the covers on the bed and slipped into her flip-flops. As she closed the dorm door behind her and headed down the hall, the elevator doors opened. She opened the stairway door and passed through it before the elevator inhabitants exited. She had a feeling it was Tommy's family. None of the dorm residents ever used the elevator.

Cindy knocked on Tommy's door and entered, with her parents and Jamie following behind. She called out for Tommy, but heard the shower running as she stepped into his bedroom, and looked at her watch. "I guess we did make good time, Dad. We're 20 minutes early. I told him we'd be here at 10:00."

Ed and Mary took a seat on the love seat they had offered when Tommy headed off to college. Mary noticed the collage of family photos on the wall to her left. Cindy's eyes inspected Tommy's bedroom from the doorway, and appreciated that he had taken the time to straighten the bed covers and that his room was in order. Jamie saw a pair of lacy panties under the bed and broke out in a smile. The bathroom door opened and Cindy called out a "hello" to let Tommy know they were here. His hair was wet and askew and his towel barely met as it wrapped around his waist.

"You're early!" Tommy exclaimed, looking around the room.

"What kind of greeting is that?" asked Cindy.

"Uh, sorry. Let me get dressed. I'll be right out, and we'll greet proper-like." Tommy smiled at them and shut the bedroom door. They heard dresser drawers and the closet door opening and shutting and a few minutes later Tommy emerged, dressed and combed. Jamie noticed the wet towel tossed onto his bed had blocked the view of the panties, and smiled at his nephew's luck. Tommy made the rounds, shaking hands with his grandfather and Jamie, and hugging his grandmother and mother. "Thanks for making the trip. You must have got up early."

"Earlier than you, evidently." remarked Ed with a smirk. "Ready for your graduation?"

Tommy smiled at his grandfather. "Ready."

When Tommy graduated from high school he was awarded an academic scholarship at Indiana State. He confided in his Uncle Jamie that he really wanted to go to college to get a teaching degree, but was afraid the scholarship wouldn't cover all of his expenses, and he knew his mother couldn't afford any of the costs. Without hesitation Jamie offered to cover the rest with funds from the disability benefits he received from the military. Cindy wasn't happy that Tommy would be going so far away, but she knew it was what was best for him. She realized, too, that he wanted to break away from the area he grew up in, where everyone knew his business, and the events that led to his father's death. Indiana State was a four hour drive from home, which was close enough for him to come home for holidays and special events, but far enough to allow him to start fresh. Cindy got a full time job at the police department, with the help of Kyle. He had grown quite fond of Cindy, and checked on her often after the incident. Eventually, they started dating, and since he spent most of his time at her house, they decided he should move in, rather than keep two houses. He spent his days off at the farm, helping Ed and Jamie, without accepting any pay. It was his way of making amends for Cindy's indiscretions. Tommy was happy Kyle and his mother were together. He had seen her miseries first hand, and Kyle treated her like a princess. Ed and Mary also grew very fond of Kyle, and appreciated how he took care of their daughter. With funds staying in their checking account where they belonged, Kyle's help and Jamie's hard work, the farm flourished. Ed was able to pay off a long term loan and update some of his equipment. They were all so proud of Tommy, being the first to graduate college in their family. Ed and Mary were grateful when Kyle offered to stay at the farm so Ed could take the time off to attend Tommy's graduation.

The family freshened up and changed into their dress clothes, then headed over to the college for the graduation ceremony.
They sat through speeches and ceremonies, and finally the moment came when the college president announced Tommy's
name and he received his diploma. The family cheered for him, teary-eyed, and hugged each other. Cindy whispered in her brother's ear, "I can never thank you enough. You have done so much for Tommy and me. I love you, Jamie. You're a saint."

When the ceremony concluded, the graduates collected the caps they had tossed up in the air, and found their way to family members. Tommy received hugs and congratulations from his family, who each took a turn looking at his diploma. Claire approached, and the family performed the congratulation routine all over again. Tommy and Claire had been dating for about a year, and he was crazy about her.

When they first met, he couldn't believe she was interested in him. She was quite popular on campus. It seemed there were always guys hanging around, trying to get her attention, but she stopped Tommy one afternoon in the library and asked him if he wanted to go get a coffee or something. At first, he thought someone was playing a joke on him, but they ended up spending the afternoon in the coffee shop and found they had a lot in common. He got up the nerve at the bottom of his third cup to ask her to go to the movies that Friday night, and they started dating from there. She was his first true girlfriend. He had kept to himself in high school, and never got involved with any sports or other activities after school as he felt obligated to return home as soon as school let out for the day. He felt his father was less apt to abuse his mother if he was around. He preferred to take a beating himself over hearing his mother suffer, and stifling her sobs in the night. Claire had accompanied Tommy on his last few visits home, and everyone, especially Cindy, took a great liking to her. As Tommy had explained to his mother before bringing her home the first time, Claire had no family. She never knew her father and had been raised by her mother who was a professor at Indiana State. When Claire was a senior in high school her mother was diagnosed with cancer and died within six months. The college staff took Claire under their wing, allowing her to stay on campus and attend classes with no tuition. She also earned her degree in education, graduating at the top of their class.

The family went to a local restaurant for a celebratory lunch with Tommy and Claire. Ed offered a heartwarming toast to the futures of two very special young adults, and Cindy toasted Jamie for his help with Tommy's education. Mary attempted to take family photos, but spent more time fighting with her camera settings than snapping pictures. They finished dessert and Ed reminded everyone they had a long drive back home, so they sadly started with their goodbyes to the guests of honor. Cindy made arrangements to pick Tommy up in a week or so, whenever he was ready, and the family piled into her car for the ride home. Tommy had to wrap up a few formalities and had an appointment with some of the staff members to discuss his plans for the future. He had to clear out his dorm room and pack up his belongings.

As they pulled away, Tommy gave Claire a big bear hug. "You know how much my family loves you?"

Claire smiled up at him and asked, "No, how much does your family love me?"

"Almost as much as I do." They kissed and walked with arms around each other into the dorm. Claire had found a stash of cardboard boxes and started filling them with the winter clothes that had made their way to the back of Tommy's closet once the warmer weather arrived. He ordered a pizza for dinner and they opened a couple of beers from his mini-fridge and ate in front of the T.V. They heard parties going on in the rooms around them, but preferred just to hang with each other. It had been a long day, so they finally made their way to Tommy's bedroom. He picked his towel, still a bit damp, from the bed.

"Sorry 'bout that." He hung it in the bathroom and returned to find Claire on his side of the bed against the wall, fast asleep. He knew her peaceful sleep wouldn't last long. It rarely did.

In the dead of night, a few hours later, Tommy was awakened by Claire's stirring. Her legs twitched and she whimpered, then awoke with a start. She looked over at Tommy to see if he was awake or asleep. He was laying on his side, head propped up on his bent arm, smiling at her. "Did you see her?" he whispered. Claire smiled sweetly and shook her head yes, then turned to face him.

"Yes, and she was so beautiful, dressed in a white dress for my graduation. Her hair was up in a twist and she had one of her wide brimmed hats on. She told me she was so proud of me, and she told me she likes your family very much. She appreciated that they included me in your celebration. She said we have great plans ahead of us, and she knows we can make it work. She held out a long stemmed red rose, but when I reached for it she started to fade away. I moved forward and she just kept getting farther away. I ran to catch her, but then she was gone." Claire's face turned sad.

Tommy brightened her back up, "But you got to see her again, and she is very proud of you." Claire's smile returned and she reached out to comb his hair with her fingers, then curled up and closed her eyes, hoping to fall asleep quickly, and maybe to catch up with her mother. She missed her terribly, but was comforted by the time they shared in her dreams. She felt her mother watched over her now as she did when she was alive, and just as in their past, Claire did everything she could to please her.

The early morning hours brought rain showers that danced on the windowsill and spat at the sleeping graduates through the screened window above the bed. Tommy climbed up and pulled the window down just enough to let some air in without showering them any further, but there was no use trying to go back to sleep. They had a big day ahead of them. Tommy had asked for an appointment to meet with the Career Counselor and the Director of Human Resources, and had asked to include Claire, as they wished to make a joint presentation. They had gone over all of their materials before graduation, but Claire wanted to review everything again before they met with the university staff. Tommy jumped in the shower while Claire went over everything one last time. She left the file out for Tommy to review and headed back to her place to shower and change.

She was heading up the sidewalk to her building when a car pulled alongside her. She gave a quick glance over her shoulder and tried to keep her face from showing her dread. The car moved slightly ahead of her and the passenger window lowered. "Just getting home, Claire?" asked the woman behind the wheel.

"Good morning, Mrs. Bernie." Claire avoided the question.

"I looked for you after the ceremony yesterday. Thought we might have a lunch in Terre Haute." That sing-song high pitched voice always set Claire on edge, like nails on a chalkboard.

"Oh, I didn't see you either. I was invited to join Tommy's family for a luncheon. I'm sorry I missed you."

"Tommy's family, I see. And where did the farming family take you to lunch, Big Daddy's Diner?" Claire shuddered. She wished, just once, she could tell Mrs. Bernie exactly what she thought of her, that she saw through that sickening sweet act Mrs. Bernie put on whenever strangers, and especially male strangers were around. Claire's mother had been Mrs. Bernie's roommate through their college years, and had helped Mrs. Bernie get a job in Admissions once she had been teaching at ISU for a couple of years. Over time, Mrs. Bernie had become bitter over a couple of bad marriages, being passed over for promotions at the school, and whatever drama she could use as an excuse. Claire's mother avoided her whenever possible, saying the woman just had a way of making you feel bad about yourself. When Claire's mother was diagnosed with lymphatic cancer, Mrs. Bernie became scarce, which was fine with Claire. At her mother's funeral, however, Claire couldn't believe what she was seeing, when Mrs. Bernie had a melt down and through dry tears told anyone who gave her a look that she had done all she could for her very good friend. Now, Mrs. Bernie continued her tales of martyrdom, portraying herself as a sort of step-mother to Claire. Out of respect for her mother, Claire kept her feelings for this pathetic woman to herself.

She looked at Mrs. Bernie and answered quickly, "No, of course not. We went to the Black Angus. It was awesome."

The window started its upward movement to close and Claire thought the inquisition was over until it stopped partway. "I assume you have been advised that with your studies here completed, you won't be allowed to stay on campus any longer."

Claire had not yet been advised of the status of her living quarters, but knew the school had been more than generous and didn't expect anything further. She had the funds from her mother's life insurance policy to draw on for rent, but she hadn't figured out where she would move to. Before she could respond the car started to slowly move along. "I must be going, Claire. TaTa."

Claire turned up the walkway to her complex. "TaTa to you too, you evil bitch."

When Tommy had arrived at Indiana State as a freshman in 2006, he felt at a disadvantage to his classmates as he was not as savvy with a computer as they were. He had used the computers available in the library when attending high school, but did not own one himself. While everyone else was taking notes on their laptop, Tommy pulled out a paper notebook and pencil, which earned him a few sideways glances from those around him. He had to ask his uncle to buy him a laptop, and crammed an evening computer class on top of his scheduled classes to keep up. This came up in conversation, and Claire told Tommy that she also had to purchase a laptop as a freshman and ask her friends to get her up to speed with it. Claire and Tommy decided to try to start a program to prepare freshman entering college with computer skills and supply students who completed the program with a laptop of their own. They wanted to present their idea to the Career Counselor and Human Resources in hopes they may receive some direction in how they might fund such an endeavor, and if their idea was even possible.

They met in the hallway as agreed, 15 minutes prior to their appointment. Tommy had the file, and looked spot-on with his khaki pants, white shirt and a tie. Claire thought socks would have been appropriate, but she was impressed, nevertheless.

She wore a simple dress and had her hair pushed back with a headband. She felt as though they were being interviewed for a job, and tried to calm her nerves by fixing Tommy's tie, which didn't actually need any fixing.

The large oak door with gold lettering opened and Mr. Gibbons, the Career Counselor peered out. "Well, I thought I heard someone out here. You're early. Very good. Please come in." They sat at the large table across from Mr. Gibbons and Miss LeBlanc from Human Resources. Tommy started the presentation and Claire chimed in, as they had practiced. As they proceeded, Mr. Gibbons and Miss LeBlanc seemed very engaged, asking questions and nodding with approval, which calmed them both down and they continued with enthusiasm. When they finished, Miss LeBlanc said she felt they had a good plan, but funding would be, of course, the issue. She offered to contact the supplier for the school's computers and see if they could put her in touch with a laptop supplier that might be willing to work on a sponsorship deal.

She turned to Claire and advised, "I'll make a call tomorrow and see if we can make an initial contact for you. Give me a call in a couple of days if you haven't heard from me. O.K.?"

Claire had stopped breathing, and had to take in a gulp of air to reply, "Yes, of course. Thank you so much." She turned to Tommy and they beamed at each other. Mr. Gibbons stood to indicate that their meeting was over. Tommy and Claire shook hands across the table and said several more thank you's, then left the conference room.

They contained themselves until they stepped outside then Tommy picked Claire up and spun her around. "How great was that? I thought they would give us some suggestions, but I didn't think they'd actually connect us up with anyone."

"Let's not get too excited until we hear from Miss LeBlanc, Tommy. Sure does sound good, though."

"Yah, we'll wait to hear what she comes up with. So, you have anything else going on today? Wanna grab something to eat?"

"Well, actually, I was going to start looking for an apartment. It's not like I can stay here forever."

"We already talked about this, Claire. You can come home with me, and if we get this project underway, when we get this project underway, we'll find a place together, for the two of us. Wasn't that the plan?"

"Have you asked your mother about me coming home with you?"

"No, but I know it will be O.K. She's crazy about you."

"Coming to visit with you for holidays is one thing, moving in is another. You need to ask her."

"Let's go call her right now. I'm telling you, it'll be fine."

"You go call her. And don't push her into anything she isn't comfortable with. I don't want to be in her home if she doesn't really want me there. Call her and I'll catch up with you later." Claire fixed Tommy's tie again and gave him a kiss. He gave her a giant hug and they each headed off to their quarters.

Tommy got back to his dorm room and stared at his phone. He really didn't know how Cindy would feel about Claire coming home with him. He started dialing, not sure how he should pose the question. The phone rang several times and he was just about to hang up when she answered, winded. "Hi mom. Did I catch you at a bad time?"

"No, I was downstairs doing laundry. I thought it might be you. You ready to come home?"

"Just about. Claire and I had a great meeting today to propose our laptop program to the school."

"What did they think?"

"They liked the idea. They're going to try to put us in contact with some suppliers to see if we can get laptops from manufacturers. The woman from HR said to give her a couple of days and she'll let us know. Once Claire hears from her, I guess we can head home." Before his mother could respond to his last comment he continued, "I hope it's O.K. if Claire comes back with me. Now that she's earned her degree, she won't be able to stay on campus anymore. So, I'd like her to come home with me until we know what direction this project will take." He hesitated for a few seconds, then asked, "Is that O.K. with you, Mom?"

There was a pause, and then his mother said, "Well, I guess I can't tell you that you shouldn't be living under the same roof with someone until you marry them, considering that Kyle has moved in with me. Your grandparents are going to give it to me for allowing it, but I'm going to say yes, Claire can come back with you. It's not like she has a home of her own."

Tommy was so relieved. His mother had actually detailed some of the arguments he planned on using if she had said no. "O.K., great. Thanks, Mom. So, why don't we plan on next Thursday or Friday to come home. Does that work for you?"

"Thursday is better for me. It's Kyle's day off, so he can drive with me. Actually, we'll drive his SUV so we have room for your things and Claire's. I'll call you Wednesday night and let you know what time, all right?"

"Thanks, Mom. I love you."

"Love you, too, son."

Tuesday morning, Miss LeBlanc called Claire and asked if she and Tommy could come by her office. They arrived within an half hour, anxious to hear whatever she had to tell them. Her office door was open, so they tapped lightly on her door as they entered.

"Come in. Have a seat." She had been making some copies at her copy machine and carried them over to the file they had left with her in their first meeting. She smiled as she took her seat behind the desk. "So, there is a manufacturer that is very interested. I had our Purchasing Department contact them and outline a brief idea of your project. They are interested to hear more, and actually had some ideas of their own. A meeting has been set up for June 6th at 2:30, in Mr. Gibbons' office. If we can make it work, a detailed plan could be presented here to our board and we may get this thing up and running for fall semester. Are you both available on the 6th?"

They both tried to control the giddies and shook their heads yes.
"We actually have a full presentation with more details beyond the outline we laid out to you and Mr. Gibbons."

"Great. I think this first meeting will be a brainstorming mission. We'll see what the manufacturer comes up with and you can provide your further input. Sounds good."

Cindy and Kyle arrived on campus bright and early on Thursday. They shuttled the boxes out of Tommy's dorm and headed over to Claire's. Cindy was impressed that the boxes were labeled with their contents, though she noticed it was not Tommy's handwriting. Claire's mother had taught her that you can take the time to organize now or waste the time to search later. Claire was ready to go and it only took minutes to move her out. Most of her things were in storage with a few pieces of furniture and some of her mother's belongings that she kept after her mother passed. She had offered up everything else in their house to goodwill. Her mother's attorney put the house up for sale and moved the proceeds into the account he set up with the benefits from the life insurance policy, in keeping with her mother's wishes.

They returned home and started to unload the boxes. Tommy's room was small, so Cindy offered a space she had cleared in the garage where they could store anything they didn't need to keep in the house. Tommy was surprised when he entered the garage and saw that Kyle had cleaned up and organized everything so you could actually walk through without climbing over piles of broken equipment and rusted out engine parts. He even set up a shop in the corner with his table saw and some other building equipment. He had made many improvements to their house which had been neglected by Vick. Tommy headed back into the

113

house with a box of clothes and heard Cindy giving Claire a quick tour of the place, pointing out light switches and showing her down to the basement where the laundry room was. They snickered about how much laundry men produced. He was grateful Cindy was making such an effort to make Claire feel at home.

As everyone continued moving boxes into the house and garage, Jamie and Ed arrived. Tommy was up in his room and heard their voices. He ran down the stairs to greet them, noticing a funny smile on his uncle's face, with Cindy and Claire staring wide eyed at each other. As Tommy shook hands with his uncle and grandfather he looked around the room. "What's up?" Jamie nodded out to the driveway. Tommy saw his grandfather's pick up and a car he didn't recognize alongside it. He looked back at Jamie who was holding a set of keys out in front of him.

"Don't you think it's about time your mom stops driving your ass around?"

"Oh my God, are you serious?" Tommy didn't yet reach for the keys in case this was a bad joke.

"Picked it up last week. Go ahead, take the keys. She's all yours."

Tommy took the keys and turned to Claire with a look of disbelief. "Let's go see our new car." The family piled out of the house to catch up with Tommy. He was already sitting in the driver's seat, holding onto the steering wheel. Then he climbed out and circled the car slowly.

"Kyle and I been getting it ready for you. We washed and waxed it, changed the oil and checked the brakes. She's got some miles on her, but she runs like a top. Kyle cleaned up the inside and put a new set of tires on the front. She's good as new now." Jamie stepped back and said, "Climb in Claire. You and Tommy take her for a spin around the block."

They opened the doors and got in, buckling up while looking at the interior which did look and smell like a brand new car. Tommy started the engine and they pulled away slowly. They just went for a short drive. Tommy wanted to get back to thank his uncle and Kyle. As they approached the house, Ed and Jamie were just pulling away. Tommy beeped the horn and the two men gave a wave as they continued down the road. He parked the car and climbed out. Cindy and Kyle were still standing in the driveway. "I can't believe this. I don't know what to say."

Kyle smiled. "It was your uncle's idea. He paid for it. I just helped him get it ready for you." They stayed out in the driveway for a while longer, looking at the car and talking about the weather, what to have for dinner, and other settling-in conversation bits. They headed back into the house and Tommy had a flash back of Vick, sitting in the living room with the bat. He cleared the thought and sick feeling in his stomach and realized that if you allow it, time does heal wounds. He had never been happier than he was at this moment.

Tommy and Claire pulled into the parking space marked "Visitors" at 2:00 on June 6th. They had stopped for a quick lunch in Terre Haute but barely ate the burgers they ordered. They wanted to be sure they were not late for their meeting. Claire recognized Mr. Gibbons' car next to Miss LeBlanc's in their reserved spaces. "Let's go in." They each took a deep breath and exited the car.

Mr. Gibbons greeted them and suggested they set up at the middle of the conference table. They pulled their files out and got organized. Miss LeBlanc entered with another woman and introduced her to Tommy and Claire. She was Mrs. Proctor from Purchasing. A few minutes later they heard steps in the hallway and Mrs. Proctor went out to greet and direct the visitors into Mr. Gibbons' office. She introduced Bill Newbauer from Viking Technologies and he introduced Hank Breen from the Barron Scholarship Foundation. They all found seats at the conference table and Tommy started right in, thanking everyone for their time. He and Claire went through their entire presentation. The others at the table sat quietly, most impressed by the research the two of them had obviously invested many hours in. They had charts, tables and other material backing up their key points. Claire pointed out that studies revealed dedication to a product that performed well and familiarity were key factors when it came time to purchase a second or newer item. "If your first car is a Chevy and it serves you well, research shows that you will consider a Chevy when looking for your next vehicle. The same holds true with kitchen appliances, camera equipment, and now with computers. If students start with a Viking computer, they will be familiar with its operating system and consider a Viking for their next purchase over another manufacturer."

Tommy made the suggestion that to be involved in the program, which was a great asset in recruiting new students, the colleges should make a commitment to Viking that future computer purchases for the institution would be with Viking.

Claire suggested the computer skills could be taught by students majoring in computer programming for extra credits. The only paid salaries would be to Tommy and Claire who would set up the programs at each institution.

Their presentation lasted about a half hour, covering every aspect they felt would sell their idea. When they finished, Hank from the scholarship foundation commented that this was a great idea. While it didn't fall into his regime of scholarship funding, he would coordinate with another department head at the foundation. He asked Tommy how he came up with it. Tommy relayed the story of his own experience, and that his uncle had purchased his laptop for him or he would have been without, and at a great disadvantage compared to his classmates.

"You're lucky. Not everyone has a rich uncle to call on." remarked Hank.

"Neither do I, Mr. Breen. My uncle Jamie lost his leg serving in Iraq. He took the hit and saved his buddy's life. He bought my laptop with his disability funds. So, you are right. I am lucky to have him. In more ways than one." Tommy's voice broke and he was quickly embarrassed.

Hank recognized this and quickly spoke up to take the attention away from Tommy. "I like it. I'd like to go back and present it to my counterpart and our board and get back to you." He turned to Bill. "Is Viking in?"

Time stood still in the room. The clock on the far wall clicked off five seconds. "I'm in."

The meeting adjourned and another was scheduled for the group to return in 10 days. Everyone shook hands and collected their items to depart. Hank stepped aside and motioned for Tommy to join him. "Please thank your uncle for his service and his sacrifice. We are fortunate to have brave men such as him protecting us."

"Yes, sir. Thank you." Tommy shook Hank's hand one more time before he picked up his briefcase and left with Bill.

Miss LeBlanc smiled and said, "Mrs. Proctor and I will speak to the powers that be about an agreement with Viking.
It shouldn't be a big deal. I think we purchase all of our computers with them anyway. You kids did a great job. Great job."

As they headed down the hallway of administration offices, Tommy stopped and checked his pockets. "Shit. I left my keys on the table. I'll be right back." He turned and jogged back to Mr. Gibbons' office. Claire continued slowly toward the door waiting for Tommy to catch up when the door to Admissions opened. Claire caught a glimpse of Mrs. Bernie moving out into the hallway. She looked around quickly to see if there was a restroom door or stairway she could escape to, but it was too late.

"Claire, what are you doing in here, snooping around?"

Claire had no intention of sharing any information about their plans to anyone until it was time, especially this negative nelly.
"Uh, I just stopped in to see Miss LeBlanc about something. How are you doing?"

Mrs. Bernie felt Claire was hiding something, and ignored Claire's question. "Ugh, Miss LeBlanc. I can't stand that woman. Are you looking to be hired? Human Resources is not where you should start. But, believe me, this is the last place you want to look for a career. I've been here 20 years, and I'm just sticking it out now for the retirement benefits. I can't tell you how many times I have been passed over when it came time for a promotion. I know this place inside out. I could practically run the whole university, but they keep me stuck in that office. I can't stand my supervisor. He never listens to a word of my advice. I just keep to myself and do my work. When the clock says 5:00 I am out of here. They just don't appreciate me. So, what position are you interested in?"

"I'm not looking for a job. I just wanted to run an idea by Miss LeBlanc." Claire turned and looked back at Mr. Gibbons' door, wondering what was taking Tommy so long.

"I guess your boyfriend went back home. That'll probably be the end of that romance. I've seen it happen time and again. You'll each go your separate ways. Don't worry. There will be plenty more. You just need to work on your appearance a bit. Wear makeup and do something with that head of hair, and you'll get yourself a good man."

Neither of them heard Tommy as he approached. Claire had complained to him about Mrs. Bernie in the past, so the comments he overheard didn't surprise him. What was surprising was the sudden sense of rage he felt. Tommy was not one to anger easily, but he had grown up watching his mother get bullied by his father, and in later years he became the target. He stepped in between Claire and Mrs. Bernie and was about to lash out when Claire grabbed his hand and squeezed it tightly, signaling him to

120

abstain. "Oh, here you are sweetheart. Did you find the keys to your car? We really need to get going."

Tommy stifled his anger and looked away from Mrs. Bernie to get himself under control. "Take care, Mrs. Bernie." Claire tugged at Tommy's hand and still squeezing it tightly, urged him down the hall and out the door. When they got to the car Tommy punched the hood and turned away from Claire. She stood silently and let him deal with his emotions.

"I hate that woman. Why did you let her talk to you like that?"

"Her words don't bother me. She is a pathetic, lonely woman who sees everything in a negative light. Look at us. We have everything going for us. We are on top of the world. What good would it do to lash out at her? She wouldn't change. She would just add us to the list of people that have done her wrong. She has colored herself as a victim, and that is who she wants to be.
I only feel sympathy for her, not hate."

Tommy looked across the hood of the car at Claire, and at that point he knew she was who he wanted to spend the rest of his life with. He smiled. "I love you, Claire."

"Me too. Now let's get the hell out of here before she comes outside with more advice." They smiled and jumped in Tommy's car to head home.

Tommy headed out for his morning run early to beat the heat. He had started running while at ISU, and was somewhat addicted to it. He loved this stretch of the road, passing through corn fields on either side. The view changed with the seasons. In winter the snow covered fields seemed to stretch as far as the eye could see. In the early spring the fields were tilled in perfect rows, with the dark soil revealed. Once the corn was planted, you could almost watch it grow until late summer when it formed a tunnel to pass through along this stretch. In late fall the huge machinery made its way along the still perfect rows, cutting the tall proud stalks effortlessly. It smelled like home. Kyle, on his way to work, passed him and gave a quick beep and a wave through the back window. When Tommy returned to his driveway he slowed to a walk, shaking the run out of this legs. He entered the kitchen and saw a note on the table from Claire reminding him that she and Cindy were shopping and running errands for the morning, so he decided to head over to the farm and see what Jamie was up to. He took a quick shower, then headed back down to the kitchen. He wolfed down a muffin and, since no one was home, drank right out of the milk carton while holding the refrigerator door wide open.

When he arrived at the farm, his uncle was over by the garage, working on the tractor. Jamie looked up as Tommy approached and said, "Hey slick. Nice milk mustache." Tommy quickly wiped the dried milk from his upper lip with the back of his hand.

"Wassup?"

"Just fighting with a hose on this tractor that doesn't want to hold its position. Course, it has to be the hose that's hardest to reach. Your grandfather and grandmother went into town. She has a dentist appointment and he's gettin' his haircut. Hey, can you hand me that three eighths wrench from my toolbox down there?" Tommy started pawing through the box of tools. Jamie looked down to see what was taking so long. "It's the one that says 'three eighths' on the handle, college graduate." Of course, Tommy's hand went right to the proper tool at that moment, so he handed the wrench up to his uncle with a smirk. "Speaking of which, when is your next meeting back at school?"

"Should be this week, on Friday. They're gonna call and reconfirm."

"Want some company? I could use a couple of days off, and I'd like to hear exactly what this is all about, unless you'd rather not."

"Actually, that would be cool. I'll have Claire book another room. We'd love to have you there. Awesome." He meant it. This was a big deal, and while his uncle wasn't up on computers, he was very smart and clear thinking. It would be good to have Jamie there looking out for their best interest, and Claire loved Jamie, so he knew she would be excited to have him join them.

When Tommy got back home he checked his phone and a message had come in while it was charging. It was the secretary for Bill Newbauer at Viking saying he'd like to meet with them for lunch on Thursday. It hit Tommy right then. Someone's secretary just called him to set up an appointment. It looked like this was really going to happen.

Claire returned home and Tommy greeted her in the driveway to help carry bags in. He told her that Jamie had asked to join them and, as he had assumed, she was delighted. He told her they needed to change their plans to head down to the campus a day early, as Mr. Newbauer's secretary asked them to meet for lunch on Thursday. When Claire asked why he wanted to meet with them before Friday Tommy shrugged it off, saying his secretary left the message with the time and place, but didn't get into why. While she called their hotel to make the changes, he called Jamie and told him they'd be leaving early Thursday morning.

Jamie's bag was sitting out on the front porch and he exited the screened door as soon as they pulled up to the house. Claire jumped in the back seat as Jamie approached the car. "Oh no, Claire. I'm sitting in the back. Get up front."

Claire locked the two back doors and looked out the window at Jamie, shaking her head no. He slumped his shoulders and ordered her again to move up front. She shook her head again and looked straight forward, indicating that the discussion was over. He reluctantly opened the front passenger door and lowered himself into the seat while Tommy tossed his bag into the trunk. As they headed out the driveway, Tommy reached for the radio to turn the volume down. "Wait." said Jamie. "You know this song?"

Claire and Tommy both acknowledged. Claire named the band and title while Jamie offered up, "I know the guy that wrote this."

"Really? Did you serve with him?" Claire asked.

"No, I met him right when I got out. He wrote a bunch of songs after that, including this one. He ended up leaving his regular job and just writes country songs now." He turned to look back at Claire. "Maybe it's an omen, telling you to follow your dreams, girl."

"I'll take that. Turn it up, Tommy!" Tommy followed orders and they headed down the road with the morning sun shining bright as ever, radio blaring, heads nodding.

Later in the drive, Tommy and Jamie were talking away, as they could do for hours on end. Claire was in her own little world. Her eyes were closed, but she wasn't asleep. She was recalling the visit from her mother in last night's dream. They had been sitting in the restaurant where their lunch meeting with Mr. Newbauer had been arranged, just she and her mother. They actually had spent many Sunday mornings there for a late breakfast when Claire was growing up. They were sitting at her mom's favorite table, away from the noise of the kitchen, and the smell of the bathroom, but close to the counter so the waitresses couldn't help but give good service. Her mother was sipping her coffee and gazing at Claire. They had finished their eggs, and Claire was playing with the crusts she had pulled off her toast. Her mother set her cup back on the circle of coffee, marking its spot on the placemat and leaned forward to make sure she had Claire's attention. Then she said, "There are people in this world who will try to take advantage of you. Don't s...." And then she was gone. Claire had awakened to the buzzing sound of the alarm clock. She jumped up and hit the red tab on top to make it stop so it wouldn't disturb Cindy and Kyle at such an early hour.
Now she sat in the back of the car, wondering about her mother's warning. Was it just advice in general, or a warning about the project? Her eyes jumped open when the car came to an abrupt stop.

"We're here, sleeping beauty. Let's see if we can check in this early." Tommy was out of the car before finishing his suggestion.

The hotel did have their rooms ready, so they found their way and dropped off their bags. Jamie hadn't planned on joining them for lunch. He said he was just going to crash in front of the T.V. and maybe grab something quick nearby. He told them to give him a shout when they returned.

They decided to walk to the restaurant, which was only a few blocks from their hotel, since it was such a beautiful day. When they arrived, Mr. Newbauer was already seated and gave them a wave. Claire couldn't help but notice he was sitting at the table she and her mother occupied several hours earlier. The waitress came right to their table as they sat down, asking if they were ready to order. They made some small talk about the drive down and the weather. Mr. Newbauer opened the briefcase sitting on the chair next to him and pulled out a file with two thick sets of documents, handing one to Claire. She skimmed the first few sentences of legal jargon while he explained to Tommy that he wanted to meet with them to get some formalities out of the way so they wouldn't hold up the other parties attending Friday's meeting. He pulled a pen from his shirt pocket and clicked it to the writing position, continuing to explain that this was just a standard legal document protecting both of them and Viking from anyone else who might try to capitalize on

their program. Claire settled the documents on
the napkin on her lap and leaned over to view
the copy Mr. Newbauer held out to show Tommy.
As he extended his pen, he explained which
page numbers they needed to sign and which
just required initials. He offered that he had
already signed both copies. Over Mr.
Newbauer's shoulder, Claire noticed a woman
making her way toward them, carrying a brown
bag and a to-go cup of tea, with the tea label
fluttering. Tommy had taken the pen and was
about to start signing where instructed when the
approaching woman stopped at their table.
Claire looked up to see it was Mrs. Bernie.

"Good morning, Claire. I thought that was you."
She passed her glaze around the table and
continued. "Am I interrupting something?"

"Hello, Mrs. Bernie. We're just having a little
meeting here about a project Tommy and I have
been working on."

"Yes, I heard all about it from Mrs. Proctor in
purchasing. Sounds very interesting." She had
fixed her gaze on Mr. Newbauer. "But I thought
your meeting was set for Friday."

"Yes, it is. Mr. Newbauer here wanted us to sign
some paperwork before the meeting to get it out
of the way." For once, Claire was actually glad
for Mrs. Bernie's stop to chat. Something here
didn't seem right.

"Looks like a pretty important document. Have
you had time to read it over, or have your lawyer

review it, Claire?" Now her eyes moved from Claire to Mr. Newbauer. "Once you sign something like this, you can't take it back. Maybe you should take this with you and if you find it to be in proper order, you can bring the signed copy to the meeting on Friday." She stood on guard, making sure her point had been received.

"Well, I don't see any harm in that, do you Tommy?" Claire jumped at the opportunity to keep him from signing. Tommy looked at Mrs. Bernie, then at Claire.

Before he could agree, Mr. Newbauer said, "Well, actually, I'm not sure if I'll be able to make tomorrow's meeting. If we take care of this formality today, my absence won't hold anything up, and time is of the essence if you want this to be up and running with the fall semester. You should just sign it now, and you can read it later."

"Well, I've never heard of such a thing. Who would sign a legal document with intention of reading it afterward?" Mrs. Bernie's voice was not its usual sing-song sickening sweet melody, but had become quite stern and direct.

Tommy finally spoke up. "I'm sure this is a standard document that people involved in this sort of thing sign all the time, but this is our first endeavor, and I would feel more comfortable if we take it with us and bring it to the meeting tomorrow, signed. If you aren't able to make the meeting, we can send it to you."

"I'm afraid that isn't possible. If you don't sign this today, we will have to pull out of the deal. I'm afraid you are making a very big mistake." He tapped the document on the table to avert Tommy's attention back to it.

"Mr. Newbauer," Claire stated calmly, "It would be a very big mistake to sign an unread agreement." She took the document packet from her lap and set it on the table.

Mr. Newbauer's face was crimson. He grabbed the pen from Tommy's hand, picked up the two sets of documents with trembling fingers and tossed everything into his briefcase, fumbling with the closure tabs. He stood and eyed the two young people across from him and said angrily, "Good luck to you." He turned to Mrs. Bernie, glaring, and shoved past her and out the door.

The waitress appeared with their meals and everyone just looked at each other, speechless. The waitress set their burgers in front of them and went back into the kitchen with Mr. Newbauer's lunch plate.

"Thank you, Mrs. Bernie. I think you just kept us from making a big mistake." Claire said as she looked up at her.

"There are people in this world who will try to take advantage of you. Don't sign anything you haven't read, ever." She put her hand on Tommy's shoulder and then left the restaurant.

Claire and Tommy sat for a moment, then Tommy said, "I guess we better call Miss LeBlanc when we get back to the hotel."

They ate in silence, then started their walk back. Claire told Tommy about her dream the night before. "I actually got a chill when Mrs. Bernie said the exact words of my mother last night, finishing the sentence she was in the middle of when the alarm went off. How freaky is that?"

"Freaky. Very fuckin' freaky." was Tommy's only reply.

Tommy called Miss LeBlanc's office and she picked up on the fourth ring. As he started to tell his tale, she interrupted him. "Tommy, no worries. I just got off the phone with Hank Breen at the Barrett Foundation. Evidently Mr. Newbauer called Hank to tell him the deal was off. Hank made some calls and has another laptop supplier chomping at the bit to take part. He's made arrangements to have them join us Friday. I'm not sure why Viking pulled out, but it will be their loss." Tommy reluctantly told Miss LeBlanc about the invitation to an earlier meeting and the issue with signing the documents. As he was explaining it to her, Tommy realized how ignorant it made him sound.

"Well, that explains it. You and Claire were very smart not to sign that document. I have to wonder what was in it, but I am very impressed that you didn't let him coerce you into signing."

Tommy was relieved at her positive spin. "So, we'll see you on Friday."

Tommy smiled as he ended the call and turned to Claire. "Guess we're back on track. Let's check on Jamie and see what he's up to."

They went to Jamie's room and told him the events of their lunch meeting. Claire left out the part about her dream, but once they had finished with the whole story, Tommy added, "And you know what's weird? Claire had a dream about her mom last night. Well, Claire, you should tell Jamie. It was your dream. Tell him."

Claire hesitated. "It was just a dream. It's silly, really."

Jamie gave Claire a gentle smile. "Tell me, please."

Claire started slowly explaining that she had frequent dreams of her mother, and then continued with the description of her dream the night before. She wasn't comfortable in relaying something so intimate to Jamie, but he smiled knowingly and her confidence grew. He told her about his Uncle Gus who came to visit him during the night, though he wasn't always sure if it was real or a dream. "In fact, my Uncle Gus is the reason I'm on this excursion with you. He told me I should come." Jamie admitted with a shrug. She felt settled with his admission, and continued by telling him that some nights she watched the clock, looking forward to getting into bed and anxious to find sleep, in hopes of another visit.

Claire wasn't aware if her mother visited her that night. She slept sound and peacefully until morning. She awoke before the alarm and pulled the covers over her shoulder, not quite ready for the day to start. She thought about Jamie's Uncle Gus, and somehow knew that even if she didn't dream about her mother, she watched over and was with Claire everyday.

It was the day of their meeting. Tommy, Claire and Jamie met in the hallway to head out to breakfast. They didn't walk this time, but drove over to the restaurant of their lunch appointment the day prior, as they would be continuing on to the college after breakfast. As fate would have it, the "best table to be seated at" was the only table available when they entered the restaurant. No noise from the kitchen, no smell from the restrooms, and right near the counter so the waitresses couldn't help but give good service. When the waitress delivered their food she hesitated before setting Jamie's down, then commented, "Wasn't sure if you was stayin' after they chased the guy out at lunchtime yest'day."

They arrived at the administrative building a little early, but there were several cars in the lot, so they decided to head in. They took their time so Jamie could make it to the door at the same time as them, though Tommy wanted to run up the stairs two at a time. As they travelled the corridor, Jamie stopped at a restroom door and said he would join them shortly. They continued to the open door of Mr. Gibbons and entered. In the collection of people gathered they recognized Mr. Gibbons, and Miss LeBlanc of course, with Mrs. Proctor from Purchasing talking to Hank Breen from the scholarship foundation. There was a man they didn't yet know speaking with Mr. Breen and Mrs. Proctor. Claire and Tommy assumed this was the representative from the laptop supplier. Off in the corner behind Mr. Breen stood a nicely dressed couple. They smiled at the two newcomers, and then at each other. Mr. Breen noticed their entrance and turned to the couple, nodding toward Tommy and seemed to say, "That's them."

He heard the woman murmur, "He's much taller."

Mr. Gibbons turned to Tommy and Claire and rushed over to stand next to them as he interrupted the chatter in the room and announced formal introductions. He started with those they already knew, and then escorted them to those they did not, enabling them to shake hands with the people that were about to make their project possible. As they approached the couple at the back of the room, Mr. Gibbons advised, "And we are especially pleased that these fine people made the trip to Indiana State University. They have supported many of our students and programs, for which we are most grateful. Tommy and Claire, this is Keith and Kathryn Barron, of the Barron Foundation." They all reached out in unison to shake hands, and laughed at their timing. As they finished shaking hands and repeating the names just delivered to them, Tommy couldn't help but notice they were staring at him. Claire took a look at him just to make sure he didn't have breakfast on his face.

"Very pleased to meet you." offered Keith. "We've heard a great deal about you and this project. You have put a lot of work into this. We are very impressed."

Mr. Gibbons headed over to shut the door so they could start their meeting, and stopped short. "May I help you?"

"Hi, I'm Jamie. I'm looking for my nephew, Tommy. He and his girlfriend Claire were scheduled for a meeting here."

Tommy and Claire were barely able to stay on their feet as Kathryn bumped and charged her way through to get to the door. They looked at each other with confusion as the woman who looked so refined and reserved threw her arms up in the air and called out Jamie's name as she disappeared past Mr. Gibbons and out his office door. Keith excused himself and also headed past them, toward and then out the door. Hank explained to those left in the room, especially Tommy and Claire, that when he returned to the foundation to discuss the project, he relayed the story of Tommy's uncle who had supported him through school with his veteran's disability benefits which had resulted from losing a leg in Iraq. He said Kathryn had asked him, "The uncle's name didn't happen to be Jamie did it?".

Hank continued, "I recalled and confirmed that yes, actually, his name was Jamie. I tried to relay that I remembered his name when Tommy mentioned it as my friend growing up was named Jamie, but Mrs. Barron didn't seem to hear much that I said after that. She called her husband immediately and told him that she had found Jamie. From then on they told me to do whatever I needed to get this project funded." He turned to the laptop supplier and nodded in his direction, adding, "Keith actually made the call to include MKN Computer Systems in this deal. And we appreciate their support with such last minute notice."

Keith re-entered the room and apologized. "You can go ahead with your meeting. Hank knows we approve of all of the plans. We're going to head outside so we don't disturb you any further. We have some catching up to do with a good friend."

Jamie waived through the doorway as his friends moved him down the hallway, all talking at once.

Jamie, Keith and Kathryn headed out of the building and Kathryn spotted a picnic table across the parking lot near a small grove of aspens. "Let's sit over there and we can catch up."

"Oh, Jamie, it is so great to see you! We were looking forward to meeting your nephew and hoped he could get us in touch with you, I couldn't believe it when I heard you at the door.

You look great! How are you doing?" Kathryn asked as they approached the table. She immediately regretted her suggestion of the picnic table as Jamie moved around it, but he sat on the end of one of the benches and swung his legs around and under the table with ease.

"I had no idea your foundation was the one my nephew kept talking about. I'd have told them to pad the bill and ask for a big salary!" Jamie smirked at Keith before answering Kathryn's question. "I'm great. Been working with my father on my parents' farm and stayin' out of trouble. How about you? I've been hearing some of your new songs on the radio. Got some good stuff out there, Keith."

Keith smiled. "I've been very fortunate. Got hooked up with some talented singers that make my lyrics sound good." He nodded in his wife's direction. "Someone's gotta pay the bills."

Jamie turned to Kathryn, "The foundation's going well?"

"Yes, thanks. It's everything I had hoped it would be. Lotta work, but I have a great staff and some very loyal volunteers. Actually, we are very intrigued by this project. We're looking forward to working with your nephew and Claire. Depending on how it goes, we may consider employing them on a permanent basis to work with institutions on some programs outside of traditional scholarships. Do you think they'd be interested?"

Keith interrupted, "This is just an idea we're working on, nothing we could offer them right now."

"I understand. I think it's best to see how they do with this project first. They're young, but they're pretty clear thinking and ambitious. Neither of them were dealt an easy hand, but they turned out pretty good so far. Let's see what happens."

Kathryn smiled at Keith. Jamie asked, "How's Kim and Brent?"

"Very well. Thanks for asking. My sister is still cancer free." Kathryn tapped her knuckles on the table. "She runs a few programs for me, and Brent still has his practice. They moved out of the apartment building and bought a house. It's an older home, so they spend a lot of time working on it, but I think they really enjoy it. Brent is very talented. You should see the fireplace he built in their kitchen."

"And how about Missy?"

"Missy is great. She worked with us setting up the foundation and really helped to get it up and running. Then a widower was doing some consulting work for us, and they started dating. He's a very nice man. The four of us got together for dinner on weekends. After a couple of years he asked Missy if she would consider marrying him and moving out to the west coast where he has a ranch. So, she said yes. They've been out there for a little over a year now. She keeps in touch, and is very happy. We hated to see her leave the foundation, but it was time for her to enjoy her life, and his family is great. They love Missy. We're talking about taking a break to go visit them."

"That's awesome. I'm glad she found someone. Mrs. Mackenzie had told me what happened to her family. It seemed like she was just starting to come to terms with it when I lived next door."

Kathryn nodded. "When Timmy asked her to marry him we had a long talk. She actually confided that you had a big influence on her ability to move forward. She said the day she met you she realized that she could spend the rest of her life as a victim, or she could look forward. I know she would appreciate me telling you that. You left so abruptly, none of us got to say goodbye. I'm glad we have this chance to see you again, Jamie. We think of you often. I'm so glad you're doing well." Kathryn reached across the table and touched Jamie's arm. As she did so, he couldn't help but notice her hand was trembling against his skin. As he looked down to verify, he watched as the shaking fingers loosened their grip and the trembling increased. She pulled her arm back and collected her hand onto her lap, under the table, then slowly turned her gaze to her husband who was still focused on Jamie's arm.

Keith sat up straight and exclaimed, "Hey, you should come to California with us! We're just going to go out for a week or so. I know Missy would love to see you. I'm in on this private jet deal, so we can pretty much come and go when we want. Can your family handle the farm without you for a bit? We're heading out the week of Fourth of July. What do you say?"

"Well I don't want to horn in on your plans."

Before Jamie could continue Kathryn claimed, "Don't be ridiculous!"

CHAPTER FOUR

<u>Head West, Young Man</u>

Tommy and Claire dropped Jamie off at the farm. They had talked all the way home about Keith and Kathryn, their foundation and the project. Claire was going to ask Mrs. Bernie for recommendations on cheap rentals in the area. The foundation agreed to give them an advance on their salaries while they got the program up and running. Now Tommy had to tell his mother they would be moving back to Terre Haute. He knew she would already have figured they would have to live in the vicinity of the university, but she probably wasn't expecting it to be so soon. Jamie was wondering how his father would feel about him heading to California for a vacation.

When they arrived at the farm, Tommy jumped out of the car to grab Jamie's duffle bag while his uncle climbed out of the back seat. It was dinner time and his mother had a place set for him at the kitchen table. Jamie gave Tommy a man hug and Tommy called a good evening through the screen door to his grandparents then headed out.

"Perfect timing, son." Mary was pouring sweet tea over tall glasses of ice, and added a third glass as he headed to the sink to wash up. She gave him a kiss on the cheek and a sweet smile.

"Didn't know I was so hungry 'til I smelled your cooking."

Ed entered the kitchen and pulled a chair out. "Welcome home, son. Did the kids get their project squared away?"

"Yes sir. They're all set. It was the craziest thing. The funding is coming from a couple that I had become friends with when I got out of the Guard. They came to the meeting because they found out Tommy is my nephew. They didn't know I was tagging along, just wanted to meet Tommy and maybe find out how I was doing. It was really great to see them again." He looked at his mother. "They're good people. Came into some money, and became philanthropists."

"What's that?" asked Mary as she served meatloaf and mashed potatoes to the men.

"Someone who gives their money away." replied Jamie, "to charities and people in need."

"Don't get much better than that. Where'd they get the money?" asked Ed with a mouthful of potatoes and gravy.

"He wrote a country song and they put it to a movie. Then he wrote another and another. Got to quit his day job at the grocery store."

"Sounds like a country song right there." Ed laughed at his own joke.

"So, uh, he asked if I'd join them on a trip out to California week after next." Jamie let it out.

"Why the hell would you want to go there?"

"Well, they're going to visit with the woman who lived next door to me. They had become close friends. She helped them get their foundation started before she got married and moved to California. I'd like to take them up on their invitation to see her, but also to visit with Ben. He had come to see me a few times after we got out, but I've kinda lost touch with him."

Mary stepped into the conversation before her husband could say the wrong thing, "Ben is the boy you saved in the explosion, isn't he." She didn't wait for a reply. "Of course you should go see him, and spend time with your friends."

Ed looked at his wife, then nodded in approval. Jamie added, speaking more to himself than to his parents, "last time I saw Ben I couldn't help but feel there was something wrong, something he wasn't telling me. He just didn't seem right."

They finished their dinner and Jamie headed up to his room. It wasn't too late on the west coast for a phone call. He pulled the folded notepaper from his wallet where Ben had written his mobile phone number, advising Jamie to call him if he ever needed anything. The years had creased the paper and the ink had bled through the folds, but the number was still legible. Jamie dialed the phone. It rang four or five times and a woman answered. Hoping he had the right number, Jamie replied, "Hello, my name is Jamie Reed. I'm trying to reach Ben Wallace."

"Oh, yes, Ben is right here. Just a minute please."

He heard muffled voices, then Ben came through loud as ever, "Jamie! My God! How are you? Everything O.K.?"

"Hi, Ben. Yes, everything is good. And you."

"Oh, ya, good as can be expected. Where are you?"

"Well, I'm back at my family's farm, but fixin' on comin' out to California with some friends and thought I might look you up,"

"No shit? Absolutely! Get your ass out here! You're welcome to stay with me if you'd like, your friends too!"

"I'm pretty sure they're all set, but I might take you up on a night or two. Probably be week after next. I'll get the exact dates and give you a ring back. Give me your address and I'll figure out how to get there."

"I'll come get you if need be. Where you flyin' into?"

"I'm not sure yet. They're making the arrangements, but as soon as I know I'll let you know. It'll be great to see you, man. And, I can't wait to meet your family. Your kids must be gettin' big. Bet that baby isn't a baby anymore."

"I, uh, I'll look forward to your call."

"O.K., Ben. Good to hear your voice. I'll call you in a day or so."

"I'll be here, buddy."

Two weeks later Jamie was headed to California in a private jet with Keith and Kathryn. Keith had made all the arrangements. He had booked rooms for them at a resort outside of San Diego. Missy and her husband would be joining them. Then a driver would bring Jamie to Ben's house which was a couple of hours away, and bring him back the next weekend so they could fly back east together. Keith wouldn't accept any money from Jamie, though Jamie put up a good fight. They were served dinner on the flight, so when they arrived at the resort they agreed it had been a long day and headed to their rooms. Missy and her husband would be arriving at lunchtime the next day.

That night, Jamie awoke to what sounded like someone clearing his throat, right in his room. It took him a second to recall where he was and to get his bearings. He saw a dark shadow at the foot of his bed, and whispered, "Uncle Gus?" As he leaned forward and sharpened his eyes, the shadow faded away. Jamie smiled, and pictured his uncle in a Hawaiian shirt with sunglasses and a straw hat. "Goodnight, Uncle Gus."

The next day he rose early and met up with Kathryn and Keith for breakfast out on their patio overlooking the Pacific Ocean. It was an amazing setting. He couldn't believe he was there.
"More coffee, Jamie?" Kathryn asked as she reached for the decanter at the center of the

table. Jamie gave a nod and held his cup up.
Katherine started pouring but lost control of the
hot dark stream as her hand trembled fiercely.
As coffee spattered the white linen tablecloth,
she attempted to halt her action. Keith
immediately reached across the table and
released the decanter from her loosening grip.
"Guess it was heavier than I thought. I'm sorry,
Jamie, did I burn your hand."

"Oh, not at all. I'm fine." He couldn't help but
notice Keith's shoulders slumping as he looked
across the table at his wife. Jamie pushed his
chair away from the table. "Actually, I'm pretty
full, and there's a comfortable looking chair over
there calling out my name, if you'll excuse me, or
better yet, join me."

Keith smiled at Jamie as he started up from his
seat and replied, "We'll be right over." Jamie
made his way to a group of lounge chairs
surrounded by a stone wall covered in a
cascade of bougainvillea, and eased himself
down on the first cushioned seat. He could hear
that his friends were conversing in a whisper,
and tried in earnest to focus on the sounds of
the waves hitting the shore, turning his head to
view the ocean. He couldn't help but remember
the day of Tommy's meeting at the school when
he reunited with Keith and Katherine, and how
her hand had trembled from control when she
reached for his arm. He wondered if he had
been witness to two unrelated occurrences, or if
it was worse than that. He had a bad feeling,
and was sorry to be intruding.

Keith soon joined him, commenting on the weather and said Katherine wanted to head inside and give Missy a call. The two men sat in silence. Jamie thought about how picture perfect this scene would look in a photo album of your life. In viewing this snapshot, one would think all was right with the world, though it seldom is.

A butler appeared, clearing away their breakfast dishes and providing them with a large pitcher of freshly squeezed lemonade. Keith's head turned as he heard his wife thank the man graciously. She approached her husband with a smile and announced, "I called Missy. She and Tim are about a half hour away. They're going to freshen up after they check in and meet us for Bloody Mary's at the outdoor cafe near the main pool at noon. I feel like taking a walk on the beach. You boys going to be O.K. unsupervised while I'm gone?"

Jamie smiled up at Katherine. "I'll be good, but I can't speak for your husband."

She smiled at Keith. "Try."

After she departed, Keith let out a big sigh. "We were hoping it was stress. She's been working too hard since Missy left. I thought this little trip would help. Guess we'll be setting up some appointments, but I'm afraid our lives are about to take a big turn here. I hope it isn't what I'm thinking it is. My cousin's husband has Parkinson's, and I remember it started this way. You know there's no cure. I hope and prey it isn't that." Keith paused, reflecting on their joint efforts that moved them to this high point in their lives. For now, he was paused at the crest of his hill. It is a good thing we can't see too far down the road.

"I hope it isn't, too."

Keith looked at Jamie's leg and asked, "why do bad things happen to good people?"

Jamie looked over at his friend, but it was a question with no answer. He thought about the journey of his life and the journeys of those he shared it with. For some, the journey was a country road, pretty easy to navigate if you take the time to slow down for a twist or turn, and offering up some colorful scenery along the way, if you take the time to notice. For others it is a stretch of highway, moving too fast, but an easy trip if you don't let yourself get sidetracked. Some journeys take place along a bumpy road with potholes where you least expect, while others offer a smooth paved surface, though the traveler may not appreciate their fortune. Some people look for an easier route, though they may get lost taking a short cut. Others are more direct, hoping to get ahead of everyone else. Jamie thought to himself that if he could go back and start his life's journey again, he wouldn't change his course one bit. He loved his life with all he had been given, and all that he had learned along the way.

The morning passed quietly, each man with his own thoughts. The warm sun lolled Jamie to such a state that he couldn't tell if he was asleep or not. A thunderous snort escaped, startling him awake and affirming that yes, he had indeed been asleep. Keith chuckled, "Scared the shit out of me. I thought we were having an earthquake."

"Yah? Well you might want to wipe that drool off your chin, before your bride returns, fool."

Katherine returned, smiling at their chuckles. "Let's go meet up with Missy."

Jamie's previous negative feelings about Katherine's trembling hands diminished as he watched her reach down to pull her husband up off the comfort of his lounge chair. She playfully wiped his chin and they all laughed again. Maybe it was just stress.

Jamie was looking forward to seeing Missy again, but he was more excited to spend time with Ben. They had formed such a strong friendship while serving. Jamie didn't have a brother, but he thought that he couldn't love a brother anymore than he loved his National Guard brother. He was counting the days until their reunion.

As Keith, Katherine and Jamie headed to the poolside table reserved for their luncheon, Missy appeared with her husband. She made the rounds with hugs and kisses, introducing Timmy to Jamie. They took their seats, all commenting on their beautiful surroundings and thanking

Keith for hosting them and making the arrangements.

As the waiter handed them menus and finished pouring their waters, Timmy raised his glass and offered up a toast to friendship, adding that he was so glad they were all able to get together, as Missy spoke of them often. They had a nice long lunch sharing stories with Timmy and catching up. As the afternoon approached they decided to adjourn for a siesta. Keith had arranged for a sunset dinner cruise and they agreed on the time and place to meet back up.

When Jamie returned to his room, he headed out to the balcony with a book and a beer. He was thinking about Missy and Timmy. He was so glad she had met someone who loved her so much, recalling her demeanor when he first moved into The Commons. She seemed so fragile, but he watched her grow stronger and begin to appreciate her own life. He wondered if he would ever find someone to share his life with. He didn't have many opportunities once he enlisted, and he knew that his disability would require a special woman. He closed his eyes and allowed himself to relax and take in the smell of the ocean and the warmth of the sun. Life was good.

It was Saturday morning and the five friends were finishing breakfast and one last cup of coffee before parting ways. As much as they had all enjoyed their time together, they were all anxious to get going. Timmy's son and wife were expecting their first child and Missy was

having a baby shower the next day. Keith's
driver was scheduled to pick up Jamie and bring
him to Ben's, while Keith and Kathryn were
going to spend the next few days house hunting.
A home in California had been on their wish list
for years. They had been working with a local
real estate agent to show them a few of the
places she had been suggesting through emails
when they set this trip up.

As they all headed to the lobby, Timmy hung
back and took Jamie's elbow in his hand,
stopping him. He held out a card on which he
had written his mobile phone number. "Jamie, I
want you to take my number and keep it
somewhere. I served in Nam in the late 60's.
When I got out, I was just grateful to be alive
and back home. My father-in-law had served in
World War II with two of his brothers. One of
them had offered to me that he was available to
talk if I should ever feel the need. At the time, I
didn't think it would ever be necessary, but over
the years I found myself becoming cynical and
angry. My wife reminded me of her uncle's offer
and, thankfully, I took him up on it. I went to his
house for lunch every Wednesday for quite a
few weeks. Sometimes he would have some of
his Navy buddies there and sometimes it would
just be the two of us. I don't know where I would
be today if it wasn't for that man. He's gone
now, but I tell you, sometimes I feel like he's with
me, watching over me. Crazy." He returned his
attention to Jamie. "No one knows the hell of
war unless they've been there and lived through
it." Still grasping Jamie's elbow Timmy put his
other hand on Jamie's shoulder, facing him eye

to eye. "You ever need to talk to someone son, you dial that number. No matter if it's day or night. I'll answer it." He then released Jamie and stood at attention, honoring the younger veteran with a sharp salute. Jamie returned the salute and holding the card tightly in his left hand, shook hands and held eye contact with this man of true spirit. Timmy then turned and put his arm around Jamie's shoulder and they caught up with the rest of the group.

Keith introduced his driver, Spencer, to Jamie as his duffle was loaded into the black sedan. Everyone said their last goodbyes and parted ways. As Jamie sat in the back seat of the sedan, he reminisced about the events and conversations of the last few days and allowed himself to get excited about the next. He had placed Timmy's crisp white card in his wallet, alongside the tattered notepaper from Ben. Now he had two brothers.

Jamie's head jerked back and he awoke, realizing he had nodded off. He looked out the window as if it would indicate where he was and how long he had been asleep, though the passing scenery was, of course, all foreign to him. He looked ahead and saw the smiling eyes of Spencer. They nodded to each other, indicating from Jamie a silent, "guess I fell asleep" and a non-verbal reply from Spencer of "yes, you did". Then Jamie turned to his left and recalled a visit from his uncle during his brief nap. Uncle Gus was sitting right next to him, dressed in a black suit with a crisp white shirt and black boots that looked worn but properly shined up. In his hands was a single long stemmed rose. He turned his gaze toward Jamie and placed the rose between them on the car seat, and then Jamie's head jerked abruptly ending their visit, and he was awake, exchanging glances in the mirror with the driver.

As they cruised slowly down Chelsea Lane, looking for Ben's address number 198, Jamie looked at the houses, built too close together by a farm boy's standards, but all nicely kept. People were outside mowing or watering their green patch of grass, or washing their car in the short paved driveway. The car slowed and Jamie saw 198 on the mailbox of a small white house with black shutters and a one car garage to the side. They pulled in and the front door immediately opened as Ben jumped out and shuffled down the front steps. The sedan had just come to a stop and Ben was reaching for the door handle. "Right on time, my man, right on time."

Ben then stood patiently while Jamie maneuvered his way out of the back seat and stood to greet his friend who was wrapping himself around Jamie like a bear. "Hey, man. Right on time but I thought you'd never get here. How the hell are you? Still ugly as ever, I see." Ben teased Jamie, though it looked as though Ben's eyes were filling up a bit.

"At least I still have all my hair." Jamie replied.

Then he looked over at Spencer, the driver, who lifted his cap from his bald head as he fetched

Jamie's duffle out of the trunk. Jamie chuckled nervously as Spencer shut the trunk. He walked up to Jamie with the bag then broke out into a huge smile. His white teeth shined brightly against his dark skin. "Got it where it counts, all's I'm sayin'." He held the bag out and Ben took hold of it. "Just call Mr. Keith when you need me to pick you up. We'll see if this bald head can find its way back here." Spencer reached out for a thumbs-up, tug handshake with Jamie. "Stay out of trouble now." He nodded to Ben with a smile and returned to the driver's seat. They waved as he pulled away from the driveway and Ben nodded toward the house as an invitation.

They entered the house and Ben tossed Jamie's duffle through an open doorway off the living room. "Let's grab us something to drink and head out back. I'll get the grill going and we can cook up some burgers." Ben grabbed two beers from the fridge and handed one to Jamie, then headed out the kitchen door to the back yard. Jamie was surprised to see a pretty good sized yard out back, fenced in and with an in-ground pool. They sat at a picnic table, popped open their beers and gestured a toast. The beer tasted good after the long morning drive. Ben started firing off questions to Jamie, asking him about the farm, who was Spencer's boss, asking Jamie if he kept in touch with any of the other guys, one after the other. Jamie was about to ask Ben where his family was when they heard a car door shut out front, and Ben turned his attention to the gate that was about to open.

A second or two passed when they heard a woman screaming, "Bert, no. No, stop! Stop! Bert!"

Ben stood up as Jamie rose from the end of the picnic table bench, automatically heading toward the gate. Jamie heard Ben's voice behind him yell once, "Jamie, don't..." It was too late. In a flash Jamie saw a dark blur hurling over the top of the gate, heading right for him. As the blur came into focus, he saw large white teeth lining an open jaw. He braced for impact, but merely felt a gust of wind with some fur brushing his face and shoulder as it passed by. He turned with the movement to see the whitewater splash in the quake of the beast. It came up quickly and dog paddled its way to the steps at the far end, climbed out and flooded the air with spray as it shook from head to tail, then sat panting, looking at Jamie, who was just starting to breath again. He heard the gate unlatch and turned back to see it fly open as a young woman burst into the back yard. He stopped breathing again. In front of him was the most beautiful woman he had ever seen. She had her hair pulled back loosely, no make-up and jeans with holes in the knees. When she moved her attention from the panting dog to Jamie, her eyes seemed to look straight into his soul. He still wasn't breathing.
Ben never told him his wife was so beautiful. She smiled shyly and approached Jamie, right hand extended. She shook his hand with a firm grip and offered, "So much for first impressions. I'm Rose, Ben's sister. I guess you've met Bert."

Jamie took a breath so he could reply. Somewhere between how do you do and hi, I'm Jamie, he came up with, "I'm how do you do."

"What a great name." Rose laughed. "What do your friends call you?"

"Jamie." he replied, red faced.

"Not anymore." called out Ben, "You're Howdy Doody from now on buddy." Everyone laughed, while Bert let out a loud bark. "Grab yourself a beer, Rose, and join us. I'm going to put some burgers on."

"I'll take you up on a burger, but it's a little too early for me and a beer." Rose sat down next to Jamie and the dog galloped over to lay down behind her. She put her hand on Jamie's arm, and said "I am glad I have the chance to meet you face to face and thank you for saving my brother's life. These words can't do justice to tell you how I feel, but I want you to know how grateful our family is to have Ben here with us, and I am so sorry that you had to sacrifice your leg."

Jamie looked into Rose's tearful eyes and put his hand on top of hers and said, "If I had the chance to go back in time, I wouldn't change a thing. Your brother is my brother. I have no regrets."
Ben reached his burly hand across the table and covered Jamie's, wiping an escaped tear with his free hand. They sat in silence.

Jamie looked at Ben and broke the solemn moment. "How about firing up that grill?"

Rose got the fixings and set out some plates while the two men tended to the grill. Jamie stole a glance at Rose whenever he got a chance, which didn't go unnoticed by Ben. As they sat down to their feast, Rose grabbed a beer from the ice bucket she had brought out, looked at her wrist as if she was wearing a watch and said, "I guess it's time for a beer now."

"So, when do I get to meet your wife and kids? You didn't send them out of town just 'cause I was coming, did you?"

"They should be back anytime. Sally took them over to her parents for a sleep-over last night and she left to go pick them up just before you pulled in. The boys ought to be all sugared up and out of control when they get here. Grandma feeds them that cereal with the candies in it, then watches them bounce out the door. I think she does it on purpose."

"The baby must be getting big now." Jamie took a big bite of his burger looking at Ben. He saw Ben's face turn cold, and Rose jerked her head up.

Ben finally confided in his friend that which he had been unable to discuss in his earlier visits. He had trouble dealing with it, and didn't want to burden Jamie with his sad story. "Our daughter was born with uh, some medical conditions." He cleared his throat and took a deep breath. "We did all we could, but she didn't live to see her third birthday. She left us, and her suffering." For the second time that day, Ben's eyes released a tear.

"Jesus, Ben. I am so sorry. I remember how much you were looking forward to coming home to your family and the new baby. I'm sorry."

"Sally took it very hard." Ben continued. "When you meet her, please know that she isn't the woman that I married. She had a breakdown after Melinda passed, and she hasn't been the same since. She just can't seem to turn the page."

Ben stopped speaking, lost in the thought of that phrase. He hadn't heard it in many years, not since his grandfather had died. When he was little and something was troubling him, his grandfather would tell him that whatever was upsetting him would pass. He would tell Ben, "A year from now you won't even be able to remember what is bothering you right now. You just have to turn the page." Now, all these years later, his grandfather's words came from out of nowhere, and he thought of all the lessons he learned from that soft spoken, gentle man.

He then continued in the present. "Rose here looks after the boys and Sally when she can. They're pretty good about keeping me on the day shift at the firehouse so I can be home at night. She just has a hard time dealing with life now. Every day is a struggle. I thank God I have my Rose, to try to keep things as normal as possible for the boys."

"I am so sorry you have been dealing with this. I wish there was something I could do to help."

With that, they heard car doors banging shut and two boys came bounding through the gate into the back yard. Right away Jamie saw that they looked like two mini versions of Ben. They charged over to the table and spotted Bert who was getting up to defend himself against the intruders. He quickly realized he was about to be overpowered and all four feet clawed the cement to start his escape. He ran to the other side of the pool and let out a bark.
The boys turned their attention to Jamie, eyeing him up and down in quick assessment.

"Are you the soldier that saved my daddy's life?" asked the boy closest to Jamie.

Before he could answer, a woman's voice called out from inside the house. "Ben, Ben!"

"Introduce yourselves to Mr. Reed. Remember your manners." Ben instructed while standing to go inside. He motioned for Rose to sit tight.

The smaller of the two boys stepped forward. "My name is Craig and this is my brother, Ben Junior. We call him Junior. I'm eight and he's nine and a half."

"I'm not nine and a half, I'm almost ten. My birthday is September 14!" scowled the older boy to the younger. Craig rolled his eyes.

Jamie addressed both boys. "If it is O.K. with your dad, you may call me Jamie."

Craig looked at Junior to confirm the permission they had just been granted to call a grownup by his first name. His eyes slowly wandered down to Jamie's prosthetic as it wasn't quite tucked under the table. His eyes then slowly made their way to meet with Jamie's. "Does that still hurt?" Junior grabbed his younger brother's shoulder to halt his questions.

"Not so much anymore. When I first lost it I had to keep looking down to remind me that it really wasn't there. I guess the nerves in my legs were still sending signals to my brain." He had the full attention of both boys now. Rose had decided not to interfere, as it seemed that Jamie was O.K. with the question he was answering with ease.

Now it was Junior who asked what many grownups wondered, but would never dare to ask. "Do you take it off, like at night or when you take a bath?"

"I do take it off at night. I figure it's been holding me up all day. It deserves a rest." He smiled at the wide eyes focused on him.
"I don't take baths, but I take it off to shower. Try standing on one leg next time you take a shower. Kinda interesting, especially when you

161

close your eyes to wash and rinse your face. Gotta have good balance."

Now Craig leaned in, and looked into Jamie's eyes with the innocent sincerity only a child can offer. "Does it make you sad sometimes?"

Jamie returned Craig's gaze and looked at his brother who seemed to be holding his breath, waiting for the answer. They had grown up in a house where sadness was an everyday occurrence, and he wanted to give them some hope that they could be happy without feeling guilty for it.

"Well, boys, here's the thing. Sometimes bad things happen to us, or to the people we care about, and it is O.K. to feel sad at the time. But, we need to remember that we have all been given the gift of life, and we should embrace and appreciate everyday we get to be here on Earth. Whether you lose a leg, or your dog, or someone in your family, you still need to move forward in life and be thankful for what you have, because if we stay sad, we are going to miss out on so much. Do you understand what I am telling you?"

With that, they all heard Sally's raised voice from inside the house. "I don't want him here, and I don't want anyone staying in her room! Get his bag off her bed right now!"

Rose looked at Jamie and the two boys who were all looking at the sliding door where Ben had entered. They saw Ben holding Sally and stroking her hair, though they couldn't hear his words. Instantly Rose got up and walked over to a baseball that had been left by her dog a few days earlier. "Who wants to throw the ball? We'll play keep-away from Bert. Come on, boys. Let's go over to the other side of the pool." It was a good attempt to distract her nephews, though they weren't moving.

"I'll take a piece of that action." called out Jamie. He rose from the table and started to make his way to Rose who was heading further away from the house. He turned back to see the boys gaping at his prosthesis. "You West Coast kids know how to pitch a baseball?"

He turned toward Rose who gave the ball a good heave in his direction. With Bert galloping toward him, he backed up a couple of steps and reached straight up, catching the ball and immediately tossing it over to Junior to keep the dog moving and barely avoiding a nasty collision. Rose put her hand over her mouth in fear of what could have happened, but then dropped it with a big smile as Junior received the tossed ball and flung it to his younger brother. Bert never took his eyes off the ball, and continued to follow its route. They kept up a pretty good game, but finally Rose missed a wild throw and Bert got his prize. He swooped up the ball as it rolled along the grass and ran a victory lap around his human opponents.

Ben and Sally emerged from the house. Sally wore sunglasses to cover her eyes, red and puffy from crying. Ben escorted her over to

Jamie and made a formal introduction. "Jamie, I'd like you to meet the love of my life, Sally. Sally, this is the man that saved me so I could return home to you. This is Jamie."

Jamie saw a tear slide down Sally's cheek and reached out to shake her hand. "I'm so pleased to meet you, Sally. Ben talked about you everyday while we were in Iraq. I knew you would be a special lady. You have two fine sons here, and a nice home." His voice was soothing, Sally's shoulders relaxed. She shook her head and looked around the back yard.

"Yes, I have a lot to be thankful for." Behind the dark glasses, Jamie could see her eyes drop down to his leg and back up to his face. It could have been the heat, but he thought she seemed to be blushing.

Rose approached and said, "So, Ben, Jamie and I were just talking and I told him of the problems I've been having with the pipes under my kitchen sink. He offered to take a look at it after dinner, so I thought he might as well stay at my place for tonight. Then he can join me at the Center tomorrow while you're at work. That O.K. with you?"

Ben's gaze went from Rose to Jamie. "I guess so." Then he looked back at Rose. "Sure."

Jamie knew he needed to verify Rose's story, so he put his best acting effort forward. Giving Rose a look he commented, "I told you it wouldn't be a big deal."

"Awesome. Saves me from having to pay a plumber."

The boys were running around the pool, tempting Bert to chase them, but as always they didn't miss a trick. Junior stopped on his way by and shouted, "can we come to the sleepover, Aunty Rose?"

Before she could reply, Sally stepped into the conversation, "No sir, you may not. Why don't you boys go put your suits on and play in the pool before you get overheated running that poor dog ragged." Before she could finish, Craig ran past Junior toward the house.

"Last one in's a rotten egg!"

The afternoon passed watching the boys romping in the pool, reminiscing over the moments of humor in Iraq, and getting to know each other. Rose was impressed with Jamie's attitude, and couldn't get over the change she witnessed in her brother in his presence. Even Sally seemed to take it down a notch, allowing a few giggles to escape when Jamie teased Ben. The men had kept their sanity by playing tricks on each other, but in relaying the courses of events they seemed to recall different versions of the same story, which added to the entertainment of the listeners. Ben rarely spoke of his time in the service after he came home. When asked about it, he would reply that it was a hell he hoped his boys would never have to experience, but that he and his brothers did

what had to be done. Rose hoped this look-
back on some of the lighter moments with Jamie
would help Ben to deal better with his demons.

As the sun moved through the sky making its
way toward its resting place, Ben made his way
out to the front yard to lower his flag down the
flagpole. He folded it righteously and returned to
the back yard where Sally was handing the boys
towels and helping Rose gather empty glasses
from the table. He couldn't help but notice Jamie
watching every move his sister made, just as
she had been steeling glances at Jamie all
afternoon. He smiled, thinking this could get
interesting, then announced, "Let's go for a ride
down the coastline and go to Tony's for pizzas
and beer."

Craig jumped up and down, raising his hand, "I'll
go! I love beer!"

"You've never had any beer." called out Junior.

The younger brother ran past, holding his towel
around his waist and called back, "Have too,
root beer."

Sally gave Jamie a big smile. "Brothers."

He replied, "Brothers."

Rose rinsed the glasses and loaded them into
the dishwasher while the others changed for the
cooler evening approaching and the group made
their way out to the driveway. Jamie grabbed
his backpack for his sleepover. "Why don't you

ride with me, Jamie?" Rose called out over the boys who were bickering over who would sit behind their father.

When Jamie got himself buckled in and gave a pat to Bert who greeted him from the back seat, he asked. "Why do they want to sit behind Ben?"

"This side is the best view looking over the cliffs as we drive along the shoreline. So, if you want, you can join Bert in the back."

"I think I'm good." He smiled. "So, I have to tell you I'm not the greatest plumber."

"Oh, don't worry. I fixed the drain pipe last week."

"Seems like you fix a lot of things around here, Rose"

"Please don't take what you overheard personally. Sally is a sweet person, really. She just has remaining issues from her loss. But, you had her laughing this afternoon. That was good to see."

As they travelled along the coastline, Jamie couldn't help but feel he had known Rose forever, even though he just laid eyes on her earlier that same day. There was something so familiar about the way she moved and especially the way she looked directly into his eyes when she spoke to him. He felt short of breath and was afraid she could hear his heart beating out of his chest. He knew the point of their driving route was to show off the views of the coastline, but his focus wasn't on the landscape. They arrived at Tony's, and Bert sat up in the back seat, then put his nose to the side window in anticipation of his exit.

Jamie smirked at Rose. "Someone thinks he's having pizza too."

"Oh, you can let him out your side. Tony allows dogs to join their families if they eat out on the back deck."

Jamie shut his door and opened the back door for Bert who jumped out and then had a long stretch before following Rose up onto the deck that wrapped around the building. Ben and his family had secured a table in the corner and were talking to a tall gentleman with a handlebar mustache who greeted Bert, gave Rose a big smile, and gave Jamie a firm handshake. "Welcome to Tony's. I am Tony. Enjoy!"

It was a beautiful night and they did enjoy as instructed. At one point Rose put her hand on Jamie's thigh and told him to turn around and look at the sunset behind him. He turned around but instead of marveling at the grand finale of daylight, all he could think about was the warm hand on his upper leg. He reached for his beer as he turned back to the table, and felt his face flush as her hand did not move away. The gesture did not go unnoticed by Ben who announced, "Well, tomorrow morning is going to come early for me, so what do you say we call it a night." He threw some money on the table and pointed at Jamie who was reaching for his wallet. "Don't even think about it."

On the drive to Rose's house Jamie asked, "So, what do you have planned for me tomorrow. I heard you tell your brother you were going to have me join you at the Center. Is that where you work?"

"Yes. Rose's Nursery and Daycare Center."

"Oh. So, you take care of little kids?" Jamie hoped his lack of enthusiasm wasn't showing.

Rose laughed out loud. "No, thank God. I take care of plants. I have two greenhouses where I grow plants that I sell, and where I take care of plants for people who are away from home for a while."

"What?"

"That's the daycare part. A few years ago I agreed to take care of houseplants for a couple heading to Hawaii for a month. They were friends of my aunt, and had inquired if I could go to their house while they were gone to water their plants. They lived about a half hour from me, so I suggested that I move their plants to my greenhouse instead. It ended up working out pretty good. I repotted some that were root bound and returned them all when they got home. They told their friends who told their friends and next thing you know I had to build the second greenhouse for houseplant daycare."

"People around here must really love their plants."

"Well, yah. There are a lot of people who have invested quite a bit of money in the plants in their homes. Some are into exotics and others have huge sunrooms with small potted trees. They get very attached to their plants, but they have second homes where they spend sometimes months at a time, so they pay good money to have their plants cared for. Moving the plants can be the tricky part, but I have a van and a truck rigged with systems for securing the plants en route. I actually make more off the daycare than the nursery, which sometimes gets neglected. You have a green thumb?"

"Well, I guess so. I've been planting corn for the past few years."

"Good. Well, here we are. Home sweet home." Rose pulled into the driveway and jumped out to let Bert out of the back seat. Jamie followed her into the house which was small but very welcoming.

"No plants." Jamie noticed.

"No, no plants here. Just me and Bert."

Rose gave Jamie a quick tour of the house and showed him to his room before disappearing down the hall with Bert. As she closed her bedroom door she leaned against it for a few seconds, finally able to breathe. She hoped Jamie didn't notice her heart beating out of her chest all night. She had never met anyone like him, but had a strange feeling that she already knew him. She couldn't wait for morning.

The clock radio blared from the nightstand and with lightening speed Rose hit the button to silence the annoying commercial for the local car dealership, wondering if the announcer could actually talk that fast or if they sped up the tape. She looked at the handsome face on the pillow next to her and smiled. He was still sound asleep. She slid out of bed so as not to disturb him and headed into her bathroom to start the shower. The water had just reached a nice warm temperature when the bathroom door pushed open. She smiled and asked, "Did I wake you, Sleeping Beauty." He wagged his tail in acknowledgment and she gave him a pat on the head. When Rose and Bert finally exited her room, she was surprised at the aroma of fresh brewed coffee greeting her. She entered the kitchen and saw Jamie sitting at the kitchen table with a cup of coffee and her morning newspaper., engaged in a crossword puzzle. They smiled at each other and asked simultaneously, "Did I wake you?" Their chuckle was also in unison.

Jamie looked at his watch, "I guess I'm still on the time zone from home. Hope you don't mind that I started the coffee."

"No, I'm glad you did. It smells great." Rose opened the back door for Bert who was whining that his patience and bladder were wearing thin. "You're into crossword puzzles?"

"Not 'til today." He folded the paper up and set the pen on the table. "And hopefully not after today either."

She smiled. "Ready for some breakfast?"

"I don't really eat breakfast, thanks."

"Well, good thing cause all I could offer would be a can of tuna or some crackers." Rose poured herself a cup of coffee, and wondered why it always tasted better when someone else brewed it.

Outside, Bert gave a bark at the door, asking for someone to open it. Rose offered, "Or, you could ask Bert to share some of his grain with you." She opened the door and Bert first greeted Jamie and then headed to his empty dish. He gave Rose a look. "O.K., no need to glare. I'm getting it." She filled his dish and he began wolfing it down as though the suggestion to share was for real. She finished her coffee and turned to Jamie. "Ready to head out?"

"I was born ready."

The greenhouses were much larger than he had pictured. Actually the whole operation was pretty impressive. The morning flew by with Jamie watering rows of newborns in the nursery greenhouse while Rose and Bert tended to the older "kids" in the daycare. At 2:00, they broke for lunch at a burger bar down the road. Jamie couldn't help but notice the second and third looks he was receiving from the wait staff and other patrons as they sat at a corner table. He whispered to Rose, "Haven't seen too many one legged men around here?"

She leaned in to reply, "Haven't seen too many two legged men around Rose is more like it." They both held their positions, leaning across the table, eyes fixed on each other. Neither wanted to move away.

"Then I probably shouldn't kiss you right now."

Rose looked down at Jamie's mouth and back up to his eyes, which had followed a similar course. "Oh, I think you better."

They each leaned in a little closer, and when their lips met, they mirrored each other with closed eyes and the thought that the lips they were touching were so much softer than they had imagined. They moved away slowly, smiling shyly, neither noticing or caring that every eye in the place was on them. Rose reached her hand across the table and Jamie covered her palm with his. They were both thinking the same thing. It had taken a long time for wounds to heal, but this moment of high seemed higher than any of their lowest of lows. Someone in the kitchen dropped a glass and it seemed to start the time clock again. Waitresses went back to serving, and the other diners turned back to their burgers and conversations.

Jamie and Rose finished their lunch and headed back to the greenhouses. When they got out of the car Rose met Jamie by his door with a hug. This time, they kissed much longer and harder, and followed it up with a long embrace, as though they had been apart for too long and were making up for lost time. They worked together through the afternoon, repotting and fertilizing plants, with Bert at their feet. Jamie startled when his phone vibrated in his back pocket, as no one ever called him. It was Keith, calling to let him know there was a slight change in their plans. He and Katherine had made a deposit on a house, but Keith had to head back home for a few days on business. He asked Jamie if he would prefer to fly home with him tomorrow, or wait a week or so when Keith would be coming back to California and fly home sometime after that with he and Katherine. Jamie knew his father had been carrying the workload at the farm, and another week or two wouldn't be fair to him. He couldn't imagine leaving Rose tomorrow, but had no choice, and told Keith he would join him the next day. They made arrangements for the driver to pick Jamie up, time and place, and agreed to catch up on the flight home. When Jamie closed his phone he felt nauseous. Standing next to him, Rose had heard the entire conversation. She waited, however, for Jamie to tell her. Of course, she understood. She knew he had responsibilities back home, and was only here for a short visit, but she was already in that place where she couldn't imagine never seeing him again.

They left the greenhouse and headed for her place, making plans for his next visit to California, and how they could make a long distance relationship work. When they arrived at the house, Rose took Jamie's hand and led him down the hall, closing her bedroom door behind them.

Early the next morning, Jamie's eyes opened to see Rose by his side, staring at him. "Is it morning already?" he asked.

She frowned and shook her head yes. "Six o'clock."

Bert cried from the hallway, so Rose got up and slipped into her robe, hanging on the door hook. "I'll make the coffee while you get in the shower." She opened her bedroom door where Bert was leaning, and greeted him, "Hey, Buddy. Want to go outside?"

Keith had arranged for Spencer to pick Jamie up at Ben's house at 7:30, so Rose sat with Jamie for a few sips of coffee while Bert chomped his grain, then quickly showered and dressed. She knew Jamie wouldn't want to be late. He had called Ben to let him know he was heading over to say goodbye and that his trip was cut short, but Rose overheard him saying he would be back.

Before they left her house, Rose asked Jamie if they could say their goodbyes before they arrived at Ben's. "No need to put on a show in front of my brother." Jamie agreed and tucked a lock of her hair behind her ear, then kissed her exposed neck, laying a string of kisses across her cheek until he reached her mouth, which gave Rose a shudder. She had told herself there would be no crying, but it wasn't easy. She finally stepped back and took Jamie's hand as they left the house.

When they arrived at Ben's, Sally was at the front door to greet them. She called over her shoulder for Ben and they came out onto the front steps. Sally smiled, "The boys are still asleep. They stayed up late last night watching some scary movie. I was sure they were going to come running into our room at any minute, but they didn't." She laughed again, then took Jamie's hand. "I'm sorry we didn't get to spend much time with you, but Ben tells me you might visit again?"

Ben stepped in and smiled at Rose. "Your plumbing all set now?"

Rose sighed at her brother. "For now."

Ben put his hand out to Jamie, pulling him close, and said, "Great to see you, buddy. Sorry we didn't get to spend much time. I'm glad you're doin' O.K."

"Good to see you too, man." They did the man-hug then moved apart.

To everyone's surprise, Sally stepped in and gave Jamie a hug. She whispered in his ear, "Thank you, for saving my husband and now my boys." As she backed away she smiled brightly at Jamie. Just then the black sedan made its way in the driveway.

Jamie looked at Rose, and she reached for his hand. "Call me tonight when you get home."

"Will do."

Spencer picked up Jamie's bag from the sidewalk, and tipped his hat. "Mornin', folks."

"Hi, Spencer." Jamie made his way to the car and turned to give one last waive and caught Rose wiping a tear from her cheek.

As he climbed into the seat, Spencer got in and started up the car. "You work fast, son. Broke a heart in two days? Not bad."

"Day and a half."

"Yes, sir." Spencer pulled out of the drive and they headed down the street. Jamie couldn't get himself to look out the back window.

When they arrived at the plane, Keith was already aboard, talking on the phone. Jamie made his way to the seat across and buckled himself in. The pilot looked back through the open cockpit door and asked, "All set?" Keith gave him a thumbs up and the pilot shut the door to start his take-off procedures. While Keith continued his phone conversation, Jamie looked out the window, knowing he was at a crossroad in his life. Eventually the plane started to move forward to slowly make its way to the runway. The engines grew louder which encouraged Keith to wrap up his business on the phone and flip it closed.

"Sorry 'bout that. They're working on a sequel to that movie about the Younger brothers and they want me to write another song for the Drake brothers. Course, now that the Drake brothers are up there in the charts all the time, they're looking for big dollars to do the song, so everyone is posturing. Guess that's show biz. So, how was your visit with your buddy?"

"It was good. Got to meet his family. Yah, it was good."

"What did you do? See any sights, or just hang out."

"Well, actually, I ended up spending most of my time with his sister. He's been having some family troubles, and his wife wasn't comfortable with me staying at their house...long story. So, his sister invited me to stay with her and I ended up helping her out a bit with her business, and then I got your call."

"So, is that a sunburn, or are you blushing?"

Jamie wiped his face, as if he could make his red cheeks turn back to pale. Then he smiled. "Guess I kinda, like, you know, sorta..." He shrugged.

Keith laughed as the plane's engines went from a stop to full power forward as they accelerated down the runway. As the nose of the plane lifted upward, he reached across the aisle and smacked Jamie in the chest. Both men chuckled.

Once they were airborne, the small plane climbed up higher and higher, then started banking to the left. Jamie looked out his window to see the airport buildings shrinking as the distance between the plane and the ground below increased. Once the plane had completed its turn and shifted back to a position parallel with the ground, it climbed a bit more. Finally they had reached their cruising altitude and the noise level was reduced.
Jamie cleared his ears then glanced over at Keith who was still smiling at him. "So, you going back for another visit?"

Jamie shook his head, "Absolutely."

"Well, I'll be making a bunch of trips back and forth over the next few months. Gotta work a few business deals back home and get the new house settled here." He pointed over his shoulder with his thumb back toward the airport. "You're welcome to catch a ride with me anytime you want."

"Thanks, Keith. I just might take you up on it. So, I've been wanting to ask you, how is Katherine doing? Any more of the shaking thing going on?"

"Not that I've seen, but we already contacted her doctor and he has a series of tests lined up.

She tells me she's fine and wants to wait, but that ain't gonna happen."

"You're right. Probably was stress, but best to find out." Jamie could tell Keith didn't want to talk further about it, so he changed the subject. "So, tell me about this new house."

They spent the rest of the flight talking about the new house, the music business and the dairy farm. Before they knew it, they were landing. Jamie had called his sister from California and asked if she would pick him up at the municipal airport. She was waiting in the terminal, right on time. After quick introductions, Keith was greeted by a driver and they parted ways, with Keith calling over his shoulder reminding Jamie he would let him know when he was heading back.

When they got into Cindy's car Jamie asked how everything was going. Cindy filled him in on the uneventful events during his short absence, and asked him about his trip. He told her all about his reunion with Kathryn, Keith and Missy, and then brushed over his visit with Ben, leaving out the details of Rose. He was still sorting things out in his head, and didn't want anyone to get carried away or jump to conclusions before he made up his mind what he wanted to do.

His parents were already in bed, so he quietly made his way up to his room. He shut the door and set his bag on the chair, making his way to his bed. He pulled out his phone and the folded business card where Rose had written her number. It barely rang once and she answered with "Get your ass back here."

He laughed. "Is that all I was to you, a piece of ass? You women are all alike." They both chuckled. "I miss you already, Rose."

"I was hoping you would. I miss you, too. You didn't look back as the car went down the street, but the three of us were waving goodbye like we'd never see you again. Made me sad."

"I make it a practice never to look back, but you'll be seeing me again. Actually, on the flight back to Indiana, Keith told me he would be making a few trips back and forth and invited me to fly with him whenever I wanted."

"He is very good to you. You're lucky to have such a generous friend."

They could hear each other breathing, but neither of them spoke.
Finally, Rose volunteered, "I had a good conversation with Sally after you left. Seems you made a big impression on the boys. She said when she was tucking them in after they got home from Tony's, they had a heart-to-heart talk with her. They told her they didn't want her to be sad everyday, and they wanted the family to be happy for the things they were blessed with. I told her about your conversation with them when they asked about your leg. You made an impression on them, and hearing those words from her own sons made an impression on Sally."

Jamie was at a loss for words, but this did explain Sally's whisper in his ear when he was leaving. "Well, I know it's late there, and you farm boys rise with the sun. Thanks for calling me tonight."

"I'll give you a call tomorrow night, O.K.?"

"O.K. Sleep well."

"Goodnight."

It took him forever to quiet his mind and find the path to sleep. Morning came too quickly.

When Jamie made his way downstairs in the morning, he found his father pouring two cups of coffee. "Morning, Dad. Where's Mom?"

"She decided to sleep in this morning. How was your trip?"

"It was great. Spent time with some old friends and met some new ones."

"Weather good?"

"Yah. Bright sunshine everyday. It was great."

"Sounds good. You look tired. I never heard you come in last night. What time was it?"

"I'm not sure. Somewhere after 10."

They sat at the kitchen table, sipping their coffee, talking about Jamie's trip and the farm. Jamie couldn't help but notice that his father was looking older. Without his hat, his sparse hair had just about all turned white, and the lines on his weathered face looked like a roadmap, relaying a journey of hard work and long days. Ed stood, indicating that breakfast was over. They headed out to the barn and started their daily chores.

When they stopped for lunch, Mary was at the door to greet them. She gave Jamie a kiss and hug, welcoming him home. Ed walked in and shuffled through the mail. He stopped at one of the envelopes and gave his wife a look. She stood, frozen, while he opened the envelope. Jamie watched the two of them, wondering what was going on. Then he saw a huge smile erupt as his father read the letter and looked at Mary, shaking his head up and down. "They increased their offer." She had been holding her hands, clasped together in front of her chest, and now raised them up to her face, smiling.

"What's going on?" asked Jamie.

"Well, son, the Carter family from the dairy farm next to ours had contacted me a while ago asking if I'd be interested in selling. I told him to make me an offer, figuring he'd try to lowball me and that would be the end of it. But, he made a very generous offer.
I waited a bit, so as not to appear anxious, and said I would have to think about it. He sent his two sons over last week to ask if they could

have a look around, so I obliged. I told your mother it wouldn't surprise me if he offered a little more, and here it is." He held out a letter to Jamie, trembling slightly as he extended his arm.

"Oh my God. This can't be right. That's crazy money!" Jamie passed the letter back to his father who then handed it over to his wife.

"We were going to sit you and your sister down and ask if you had any interest in running the farm on your own before we accepted any offer from the Carters. Your mother and I have been talking about spending winters somewhere warmer. With this kind of money, we can head south and I can buy you and your sister a farm, if that's what you want to do. This offer is too good to pass up."

Mary read the letter twice and then folded it back up and held it to her chest. Ed pulled a chair away from the table and sat down, smiling at his wife. Jamie walked over to his mother and put his arm around her. He turned to his father and said, "I think you better call the Carters and accept, before they change their mind or realize they typed an extra zero in that figure."
"You're O.K. with it, son?" asked Ed.

"Yah, Dad, I'm definitely O.K. with it, and I know Cindy will be, too."

While Ed and Mary went into the office to make the call, Jamie sat at the table and thought about Rose. He had wondered about spending more time in California, but didn't know how to leave his dad with the farm. That was no longer an issue. Now he had to wonder if Rose would have him. He overheard his father's conversation, speaking very calmly, offering up the name of the family lawyer and giving a lot of "yes" answers. Then he heard his father place a call to his attorney and make arrangements to meet later in the week to discuss details of the sale. The last call was to Cindy. Ed invited her and Kyle to come to dinner that evening as there was a family matter to discuss.

As they came back into the kitchen, Ed gave his son a smirk. "It would be best tonight if you act as though you're hearing all of this for the first time. I don't need your sister getting a notion in her head that you were in on this and she wasn't. Got me?"

"Well, that's gonna cost you a little extra." Jamie teased his father.

Mary served the men lunch and joined them at the table. They talked about where Mary and Ed might end up. Jamie offered that California was pretty nice, but his father shot him down immediately. "You couldn't pay me to go out there. I'm thinking Arizona. Your mother and I went down there years ago. Remember, that Grand Canyon trip, Mary? We loved it."

"What did you like so much about California, son?" Mary asked.

Without thinking, Jamie blurted out, "Rose." His parents looked at him with puzzled expressions. Well, he figured, might as well walk through the door I just opened. "Ben has a sister. Name is Rose. We kinda hit it off."

Mary smiled. "Kinda hit it off. Is that what they call it these days?"

"She's great. Has a dog, named Bert, big 'ol lug of a thing. She runs a nursery with two greenhouses. She owns her own house. She's different from most other women. She is confident but not pushy or bossy. She works hard, but enjoys her quiet time. She doesn't judge others. She's been helping her brother's family through some bad times, but she doesn't act like a martyr about it." He looked at his mother. "She's very special."

Ed broke in, "Any woman not afraid to get her hands dirty, likes animals and takes care of her family sounds like she's good enough for my son." Jamie smiled at his father. He was a tough man with a good heart.

"So, do you think she has feelings for you, too?" Mary spoke delicately. Her son hadn't had many relationships with women, and she didn't want to see him get hurt.

Jamie shook his head. "Yah, it seemed pretty mutual."

"Well, your Uncle Gus used to say that everything happens for a reason. Maybe we're all moving into the next chapter of our life."

Mary's comment reminded him of what Ben had said about his wife's troubles in moving on after their daughter's passing. He found himself repeating his friend's words, "Turn the page."

Later that day, Cindy and Kyle arrived for dinner and they all took part in preparing their meal, with the men tending to the grill, sharing a few beers and the women in the kitchen, cooking up the sides with a glass of wine. Mary had set the dining room table earlier in the day, surprising Cindy, since they only ate in the dining room on holidays.

Ed said Grace, then the silverware came to life, making music against the family's fine china. Surprisingly, it was Mary that started the conversation about selling the farm. Jamie had assumed that his father would run the show, but Mary knew her daughter would be more open to the idea if her mother presented it.

"You children know that your father has worked very hard, many hours a day to keep this farm going. He has provided for all of us with very little time to relax and appreciate the fruits of his labor. We have decided it's time for us to retire, and enjoy all that your father has allowed for us. We've been approached to sell the farm and the offer is very generous. We have accepted it."

Cindy dropped her fork, staring at her mother, mouth opened wide. Jamie held his breath, waiting for the audio portion of her reaction. He decided to try to set the tone for the sibling team.

"Oh my God." He looked at his father. "I think this is great. You deserve it, both of you." He turned his attention directly from his father to his mother, purposefully avoiding Cindy, "Dad isn't the only one who's worked so hard here, Mom. Don't sell yourself short. He took care of the outside of the farm, but you took care of the house and us. You both deserve it." Now he glanced at his sister.

Kyle had reached over to rub his wife's neck. He had been in the family long enough that he felt his comments were allowed. He, too, wanted to help direct this conversation travel a good course, and didn't want Cindy's initial reaction to be one she might later regret. "I agree. I've spent enough time here to see how hard you both have worked. Congratulations."

Cindy picked up her fork. "This farm has been in the family a long time." She was staring at her wine glass.

Now Ed broke in. "Yes, Cindy, it has. If we had more children and grandchildren standing ready to take it over, that would be the course. But Jamie here can't run this place by himself, and I don't think you or your son have the desire. We're lucky the Carters next door want to pay us more than it's worth, and are going to keep the dairy farm operation going. I see it as the best of both worlds."

Cindy couldn't argue. She just couldn't imagine not being a part of the farm. "Oh, the Carters?" Now she turned her gaze to her mother. "Where would you live?"

"We're going to travel a bit and see. We're thinking of starting with Arizona. The climate is right for my arthritis, and maybe your father can finally learn to play that golf game he's always making fun of on T.V."

"Hey, I'm not that old." Ed chimed in. This raised a chuckle from Jamie and Kyle.

Now Kyle pulled Cindy toward him. "Sure would be nice to go visit your parents somewhere warm when the snow gets to us here."

Jamie let out a silent sigh of relief. He could tell his sister had accepted the idea. She sat, shaking her head up and down, then looked around the table at her family, ending with her mother. "Smart move having dinner in the dining room so I couldn't start throwing pots and pans around." Everyone laughed with ease, and they continued with their meal. Ed started listing the things he wouldn't miss about the farm and Mary listed the things she was looking forward to in retirement.

CHAPTER 5

Never Look Back

The next few weeks seemed to fly by in one respect, with papers being signed, and walk-throughs with the Carters, determining what equipment would stay, what Ed could sell from the dairy operation and with Mary making similar decisions in the house. But, for Jamie, time dragged. He and Rose talked on the phone every night, neither one wanting to end the conversation. One night Jamie's phone rang just as the family was sitting down to dinner. He was surprised as Rose usually called much later, but even more so when he answered to hear Ben's voice on the other end.

"Hey, Bro, how ya doin'?"

"Better than you." Jamie replied, excusing himself from the table and heading out to the front porch.

"Rose tells me you're getting kicked out of your house again." He chuckled. "Gonna re-enlist?"

"No, I'm all set with that."

"Well, I got a proposition for ya. Got a couple of positions about to open up at the fire station here, and they asked me if I knew anyone might be interested. There's a grant for training and hiring vets, so I thought of you."

Before Ben could go further, Jamie admitted the obvious. "You remember I have an issue with my left leg. Might be a bit of a hindrance fighting fires."

"Wouldn't be fightin' fires. It's more administrative. I didn't get the full rundown, but I know they train you and the pay is pretty good. Figured I'd give you a call before they post it."

"It sounds good. I was sorta thinkin' about maybe heading back that way once the farm deal is done. I kinda liked it out there."

"Yah, I noticed." They both laughed at the verbal dance. "Never seen Rose like this. Didn't know she had such bad taste in men."

Jamie smiled. "Well, now I gotta come out there, just to make your life miserable. If you think this job is something I can handle, put me down."

"Done. Any idea when you can get out here? They'll be asking me."

"Well, the closing is supposed to be end of this month, but I have most everything needed to be done squared away. We have an auctioneer coming in this weekend to sell off the equipment and furniture, and the moving company is going to store everything else 'til my parents find a place in Arizona. So, I can pretty much head out there whenever they say. My father gave me his SUV, so I'd probably load it up and drive out."

"Sounds good. I'll talk to the Chief in the morning and keep you informed."

"Thanks, man. I owe ya."

"Don't start. My sister, on the other hand, is going to owe me big time for this one. That's actually the beauty of this whole thing. I finally have something to hold over her head. Talk to you later, bro."

"Later."

Jamie ran back in the house and into the kitchen where his parents were just finishing their dinner. "How's Rose?" asked Mary.

"That wasn't Rose. It was Ben." As Jamie filled his plate he shared his phone conversation, getting more excited about it as he went. His parents were in agreement that the timing couldn't be better. Ed had been wondering what Jamie would do with himself once the farm was gone.

"One door closes and another one opens." Ed said, with content.
He offered his coffee cup for a toast, and Jamie and Mary joined with their water glasses.

When Rose called Jamie later that evening she had already heard the news from her brother. They agreed not to get too excited, as the job wasn't a sure thing, but secretly it was too late, they were both over the edge. Rose asked, "What do you think about me coming out there and driving back with you?"

"Well, we'll see. I'm not sure how long it will take. I know you can't really leave your business for too long." Rose knew Jamie was right, but she was anxious to spend time with him.

"So, are you thinking of staying with me when you get out here?" There, she said it. While they both had imagined that Jamie would return and they would be together, neither one wanted to bring up the subject of living together in fear of scaring the other.
Jamie wasn't sure if this was an invitation, and hesitated with a reply. Rose held her breath, afraid she had jumped too soon.

Jamie didn't want to appear presumptuous, but realized the awkward silence was sending the wrong message, so he finally replied, "I would, if that's O.K. with you. I don't want to impose."

"Well, I'll have to discuss it with Bert. He is the man of the house, you know." This lightened the moment.

Jamie went along with it. "Tell him I'll clean up after myself and pay my share of the expenses. He won't even know I'm there."

Rose laughed. "Bert says he liked you a lot, and he says you are welcome to join us for as long as you want. What's that, Bert? Oh, he says 'just keep your hands out of his Milk Bones'."

"Sounds good. I've been trying to cut back on dog biscuits."

They agreed it was getting late and went through the routine of saying their goodnights without being the first one to hang up.

Jamie closed his eyes with the intention of letting them rest for a bit before getting ready for bed, but fell into a deep sleep. He awoke early the next morning, lying in the same position, and stiffly sat up. His phone slid from his chest and onto the quilted bedspread. He picked it up and held it in his hand, as if in some way it connected him again with Rose. As he started to undress for his morning shower he heard a car door shut and looked out his window to see Tommy heading up the walk. He knocked on the glass and got his nephew's attention, who smiled up at him when Jamie motioned to give him a minute.

When he headed downstairs, he overheard Ed and Mary telling their grandson of the job opportunity in California. As Jamie entered the kitchen, Tommy jumped up to greet him. "Dude..." Tommy smirked as he offered up a handshake hug and his best west coast accent. "California, like, wow man."

Jamie smiled. "What the hell, did you get taller since the last time I saw you, or am I shrinking?" His nephew shrugged.

"I came by to see if I can help with getting things squared away here. Mom says the auction is this weekend." He looked at his grandfather. "What can I do to help, sir?"

Ed smiled at his grandson with pride at what a fine young man he had become, especially considering the father he had been dealt. "Your uncle here has everything pretty much squared away. The rest of the work will be handled by the auction crew and the moving crew." He looked at Jamie. "I'm expecting you'll be taking Gus' canoe with you, if you can. Why don't you boys take it out for one last fishing trip on the pond."

Tommy's eyes lit up as he checked for Jamie's approval. "I'll get the tackle box, you grab the rods." was all Tommy needed to hear. They were out the door and headed to the pond.

Once their lines were in the water, the two men caught up on each other's lives. Tommy had heard from his mother that Jamie met someone when he was visiting his buddy from the Guard, but didn't let on when Jamie told him about Rose. "I can't wait to meet her. She sounds awesome." Then Tommy sat up straight.

"Got a bite?"

"No, got an idea. How about I drive out to California with you? I have a couple of weeks before all hell breaks loose with the fall semester start-up. Claire is actually spending some time with some of her friends from school down in Texas. I was going to just hang around the house, but I sure would love to do a road trip with you."

Jamie thought about Rose's offer, but he really didn't want her to have to leave the greenhouses, and this would probably be his last opportunity to spend time with his nephew before the real world set in. "Sounds like a plan, on one condition. I pay for you to fly back home."

"Yah, cool."

Strange, but while neither of them had moved, and there wasn't a breath of wind, the canoe started rocking from side to side. They looked at each other with puzzled expressions. Jamie wondered if Uncle Gus was involved, and what he was trying to say. Tommy just shrugged it off and slowly brought in his line to check his bait.

When they returned back at the barn, Mary told Jamie she had heard his phone ringing in his room a few times. He ran upstairs and saw the calls had come from Ben. He dialed him back and Ben picked up after the first ring. "You're in. Get out here soon as you can." They went over a few more details then Jamie headed back downstairs, hoping Tommy hadn't left yet. He found him in the kitchen, leaning against the sink watching his grandmother peeling apples.

"How soon can you be ready to hit the road?"

Tommy jumped from his zoned-out state. "I'm ready when you are!"

"Let's plan on tomorrow morning. I'll start packing up my things this afternoon."

Tommy volunteered, "If you give me an address, I can print out a map and the directions from my computer."

Mary stopped peeling. She was glad to see her son so happy and knew he certainly wasn't going to follow them to their retirement, but the realization that her family was going to be spread out and so far away made her heart sink. She wiped her hands on her apron and, trying to avoid any notice of her heartache, looked down at her watch and left the kitchen, as though she had to be somewhere else in the house at a certain time. Her plan worked, as the boys continued discussing their departure without noticing hers.

Ed was in their bedroom, sorting through a shelf of books he had been meaning to read, but never found the time. He turned as his wife entered, shutting the door behind her, and noticed her eyes, about to overflow the tears she was fighting to contain. "Mary? What is it, dear?" He stood to intercept her.

"I'm O.K. It just hit me, that's all. Jamie's making plans to leave in the morning for California. We're not going to be together as a family anymore." Her husband held her tightly as she finally broke down.

"We don't have to go to Arizona. We can go anywhere you want. We can go to California, or we can buy a small place in town here. As long as I'm with you, I don't care where we are." Ed hadn't spoken so sweetly to his wife in many years. He took a deep breath, trying to keep his own emotions under control.

Mary moved back, wiping her cheeks with the back of her hand.
She looked into her husband's eyes. "We are going to Arizona and we are going to have a great life. Our children are going to live out their dreams as we live out ours. It just hit me, but we'll keep in touch and I'm sure we'll get together often." Now she took the role of consoling her husband. "Cindy is with a wonderful man now, who takes very good care of her. Tommy has a good life ahead of him. We got through Jamie in Iraq, we can survive the west coast. I prayed everyday that he would come home alive. California is a piece of cake." She held Ed's face in her hands and smiled. "I can't wait to see you swing that golf club the first time."

The next morning Cindy brought Tommy over bright and early. As Tommy lifted his bag from Cindy's back seat, Jamie exited the front door, carrying straps and a rope. The SUV was packed and ready to go, with one exception. Jamie nodded over toward the barn, and Tommy fell in line with his uncle, heading for Uncle Gus' canoe. Cindy helped them secure it on the roof rack, tying it down and attaching a bright orange flag on the back grommet.
Mary and Ed came out to join them, carrying a cooler filled with drinks, snacks and sandwiches. There was nothing left to do now but say goodbye.

Mary and Cindy didn't bother to hold back their emotions. Mary had a pocket full of tissues and Cindy wore her Hollywood sunglasses to hide behind. With the round of hugs and kisses completed, Jamie climbed behind the wheel, having won the toss for who would drive first. As they headed down the drive, Jamie waved out his window, but looked straight ahead, continuing his practice to never look back. Tommy hung out of his window, waving with both arms until the SUV turned onto the paved road.

As they entered the highway Jamie was glad for their early start. There was no traffic, so he brought the vehicle up to speed and engaged the cruise control. "So, Claire is down in Texas? For how long?"

The silence after his question lasted so long he thought his nephew hadn't heard him. Just as he was about to repeat it, Tommy cleared his throat and quietly muttered, "Dunno."

Jamie waited a bit, in case there was a further response, then asked, "Why don't you know?"

Tommy looked out his window, then mumbled something Jamie couldn't understand, so he asked, "What?"

"Don't think she does."

"What happened?"

"I don't know. Ever since we finished school, she's been acting weird. Like, whenever I talked about the laptop deal and I would say 'our plan' she would correct me and say 'your plan'. Then she started talking on the phone, like going outside to talk on the phone, and when I asked her who it was or why she had to go outside to talk, she would just give me a dirty look. So, one night I followed her outside and I could hear her laughing and the way she was talking didn't sound like she was talking to a girlfriend. Then she saw me standing there and got mad and hung up. She said if I didn't trust her she was going to have to leave. I don't know. Like, I tried to talk to her the next day and she told me she wasn't ready to settle down. She said she wants to see the world, and this friend of hers asked her to come down to Texas for a while. I begged her to stay. I told her that once we got our program up and running, we'd take a vacation somewhere. So then she told me she needs time to herself to decide what she wants to do with her life. She packed up her stuff that night and a taxi picked her up early the next morning, before anyone got up. It's just so messed up. I thought we were soul mates. I thought we were gonna spend the rest of our lives together. I don't know what I did wrong."

He stopped talking, so Jamie felt obligated to offer some advice, but he didn't have any experience in this department. "I'm sorry, buddy. I thought things seemed really good with you guys. But, I guess you have to let her do her thing, and if it's meant to be, she'll come back."

"Nope. She won't be back. Not for a loser like me." Tommy turned his head out to his window again and wiped his nose with his hand.

"You aren't a fuckin' loser. It's not you, man. You don't know how many guys I served with who got dumped while we were over there. Some of them were married with kids, and the wife tells them it's time to call it quits. This shit happens all the time. It's not you. Don't ever think that."

"Well, I didn't tell Mom. They just think she's gone for a few days. I didn't want Mom to get all pissed at her, and then if she comes back..." Tommy's voice cracked and their conversation was over. Jamie reached over and grabbed his shoulder, giving it a shake.

It was their second day of driving. They were making pretty good time, alternating shifts until they decided to pull into a motel and get a good night's sleep. They had hit the road early, and had a few hours behind them when Jamie decided to stop for gas and a stretch. "You want to get us a couple of coffees while I fill her up?"

he asked as he reached in his front jeans pocket for some cash.

"I got it." Tommy waived off the offer. "Black, extra sugar, and, you want something to eat? Muffin or somethin'?"

"Sure, whatever they got." Jamie pulled his credit card out and slid it in the slot on the pump.

Tommy entered and saw the self-serve counter for coffee. As he set to work filling a large styrofoam cup he scanned the premises for something sweet and hardy to fill their stomachs. Through the window he noticed a large bus pull into the entrance, discharging a young girl carrying a sleeping baby. A backpack was handed out the door to her and the bus pulled away as she stood and watched. She turned and headed into the station, holding the door open for a man who had just finished pumping his gas. As she entered, Tommy heard her ask the attendant if there was a phone she could use for a local call. He replied that there were pay phones back by the restrooms. Tommy looked up to see her standing awkwardly with the baby sound asleep supported by her extended hip and shoulder. She stepped closer to the man behind the counter who was watching the gas pumpers through his window. "I don't have change for a pay phone, sir. Do you have a phone I might use? I just need to call my momma and ask her to come and pick me up. Won't be but a second."

The attendant continued to look out the window and replied, "Sorry. Against company policy to let customers use the phone."

The man she had held the door for brushed past her and threw some money on the counter. "Pack o' Winstons." The attendant pulled a pack of cigarettes from the display behind him and punched some keys on the register. He picked up the bill on the counter and handed the change and cigarettes to the customer who turned and looked at the young girl. He pocketed the coins and brushed past her again, heading out the door.

"Please, sir. I've run into some rough times. I just need to call my momma. I don't mean to cause you any trouble. Maybe you could dial her up and just tell her I'm here."

"Nope, sorry."

Tommy clicked the lids on his coffee cups and grabbed a bag of cider donuts from a nearby display. He set his items down on the counter and slid a twenty towards the cash register. "Got anything smaller? I'm running low on singles." asked the attendant.

"Nope, sorry." Tommy replied, looking squarely at the man, who, though he was standing on a pallet behind the counter, was a good foot shorter than Tommy. He reluctantly pulled the twenty toward him as he rang up Tommy's items, then handed him his change. Tommy pushed back one of his precious singles and said,

"Gimme four quarters." The man hesitated, then slowly counted four quarters from the open drawer and took back the dollar.

Tommy turned to the young girl and handed her the quarters and paper money he had just received. "This should help you to make that call and maybe get something to eat. You take care of that baby, now. He looks like he's going to be a biggun'." As he turned back to pick up his coffee and donuts, he glared down at the small man in front of him, then turned toward the door.

"Thank you so much. That's very kind of you." The girl shifted the baby a bit higher on her hip.

Tommy could have been that baby on his mother's hip if she hadn't tried to stick it out with Vick all those years. He pushed the door open, backing out of it and offered up, "Hard times pass. Things will get better. You take care."

As he returned to the vehicle, Jamie had just climbed in. "Good timing." Jamie reached for his coffee. "Cider donuts? Now you're talkin'."

They pulled away from the gas station and continued on their way. After about a half hour Tommy commented, "Thought we might catch up with that bus that stopped at the station."

"Did you say 'bus'?"

"Yah. The bus that dropped that girl and a baby off."

Jamie looked over at his nephew. "I think I would have noticed a bus, Tommy. I was out there pumping the whole time. No bus pulled in."

"Then you're either blind or senile, cause a bus definitely pulled in and a young girl with a baby came into the station needing to make a phone call. I spoke with her."

"If you say so."

They drove on in silence, sipping their coffees, stuffing donuts in their mouths. At every rise and corner, Tommy looked ahead for the bus. Little did he know that he had just passed the test. Just as the old man on the front steps of The Commons had done, this visitor came in the form of a young girl. Tommy had just shown his true spirit, offering to help someone in need, without being asked. How often people get so caught up in their own lives, as rich or as shallow as they may be, that they dismiss the needs of others. He felt good about his gesture, and wondered how the other men present in the station were feeling. Had they already excused themselves, or was there a chance they had a hint of guilt?

In the afternoon they switched and Tommy took over for the next several hours of driving. They were running low on conversation, so Tommy posed a question to Jamie, out of the blue. "What was the best day of your life?"

"The best day of my life?" Jamie queried.

"Yah. What was the best day of your life?"

Jamie only thought for a few seconds and replied, "That would have to be the day you were born."

"No, common. Seriously."

"Oh, get a hold of yourself. It wasn't cause you were born. It was the day."

"What?"

Jamie let out a good sigh, recollecting. "Well, as you probably know, Vick was on the road. Your mom called and said she thought her water had broke, so your grandmother jumped in the car and brought her to the hospital. My dad was milking the cows, but said he would head over as soon as he was done. I was like, eight or nine, and they knew I wasn't going to want to hang around a hospital waiting for no baby, so they asked Uncle Gus to take me into town. There was like a carnival set up on the green with a circus tent, some rides, and all kinds of animals. You could smell cotton candy when you got anywhere near town. Uncle Gus and I spent the entire day there. We ate candied apples, hot dogs on sticks, cotton candy." He chuckled. "I wasn't allowed to drink soda at home. I drank so much soda that day. They had some kinda blue soda. I don't know what it was supposed to be, but it sure was good. We went on the merry-go-round and rode these horses that had been painted with bright red lips. Almost puked on that ride. We stayed until dark when they set off fireworks. I'm sure it was pretty lame, but to me it was the greatest thing." He sat, smiling.

Tommy gave him a minute and then added, "And, I was born."

"Yah, you were. Everyone made such a fuss about you. They wouldn't let me near you at first. 'Wash your hands, Jamie. Have to be quiet in the house, Jamie. The baby's sleeping.' Finally, when you were about three months old, they sat me on the couch and said I could hold you. Your mom put you in my arms and told me to keep your head steady. I looked down at you and couldn't believe I was holding such a tiny human being. I guess that was a pretty good day, too."

Tommy shook his head, "You bet your ass. I think I was pretty cute, from the pictures."

"O.K., enough. Let's start looking for someplace to have dinner and crash."

The next morning they headed out after breakfast, hoping to make California by nightfall. They checked out the rest of their route through Nevada. Jamie was starting with the first driving shift. Tommy wasn't fully awake, and fell asleep soon after they departed. As Jamie passed a line of cars he checked the rear view mirror and startled a bit when he saw Uncle Gus riding in the back seat. He swerved a bit as he turned around, but the back seat was empty except for Tommy's bag and the empty cooler. He faced forward again and slowly brought his eyes back up to the mirror. Gus' eyes smiled back at him. Jamie smiled and whispered, "We ain't stoppin' in Vegas, Uncle Gus."

"Hmmm? Did you say somethin'?" muttered Tommy, half asleep.
Jamie sat quietly, driving on.

The Welcome to California sign on the roadside was a welcome sign, indeed. Traffic was getting bunched up as they headed up a long slope. It looked like a couple of big trucks were tying things up. Jamie moved along, but was stuck behind the climbing trucks by passing cars. He paused at the crest of the hill where the trucks were then able to pick up speed again. They were heavy with their loads of huge logs, piled up high and tied down with straps who's ends danced as the trucks accelerated downhill. At this point, Jamie couldn't see too far down the road. As they rounded a corner, Jamie saw the first truck carried the equipment used to load and unload the gargantuous trees. Just then, a pick up truck cut between the two load bearers to make a quick exit off the highway. The log carrier in front of Jamie hit his breaks, causing his rig to rock from side to side. Jamie let his foot off the gas, backing off to allow the truck to collect itself, but instead the swaying truck's movement started to swerve out of control. One of the logs at the top shifted and the heavy straps started to pop, one at a time, allowing the entire stack to shift back and forth. In a flash the

209

timber rolled off each side of the truck, knocking into guard rails on the right and turning over passing cars on the left. Jamie was hitting the brakes harder, but the wet road kept him in sync with the truck, still losing its load along Jamie's sides. Tommy had awakened and was screaming, but there were no words. The smell of burning rubber filled their nostrils. Just then, Jamie realized that one of the logs that had bounced off the back of the semi was heading for Tommy's side. He swerved toward the shoulder as the window in front of him shattered and the SUV slammed to a full stop.

Jamie could hear muffled noises, and opened his eyes, but all was black. He couldn't breath, realizing the airbag had deployed. Someone was raking at it, yelling out words he could not comprehend. There was a heavy weight on his front side and his head ached. He felt two hands on the sides of this face. "Uncle Jamie, Uncle Jamie. Can you hear me?"

Jamie opened his eyes wide, but still, all was black, except for a small white circle straight ahead. He moaned, and noticed that even his own sound was barely audible to him.

"Ambulance is on the way. Stay with me, you're going to be O.K."
Tommy shouted in Jamie's face, holding it tightly. The bright white circle was getting larger, like a flashlight shining in his eyes through the dark of night. Somehow, he knew this was it. This time was different from the close calls he had escaped previously in his life.

210

"Tommy." he whispered. Tommy moved closer, putting his ear to his uncles lips.

"I'm here, uncle."

"Listen to me. Promise me you'll watch over your mom and your grandparents. You tell them I had a great life, and I love them and you, more than anything." He tried to take a deep breath but his lungs were filling up. "Get word to Rose that I'll be with her again, I promise. You, you will do great things. I know it, and I'll be watching over you every step of the way." The light was getting brighter now. He closed his eyes, but it shined on, brighter and bigger. Dead silence now. He felt his heart slowing.
Time stood still. He smiled. He couldn't wait to ride that merry-go-round with his Uncle Gus again. He thought about the canoe, and their days fishing on that pond, with the warm sun shining down on them.

He was thankful for his journey. He was at peace.

Made in the USA
Middletown, DE
11 October 2016